. . . A Dangerous Thing

...A Dangerous Thing

A Carl Burns Mystery

Bill Crider

Walker and Company
New York

First published in the United States of America in 1994
by Walker Publishing Company, Inc.

Published simultaneously in Canada by Thomas Allen & Son
Canada, Limited, Markham, Ontario

Library of Congress Cataloging-in-Publication Data
Crider, Bill, 1941–
. . . A dangerous thing: a Carl Burns mystery / Bill Crider.
          p.   cm.
          ISBN 0-8027-3187-2
1. Burns, Carl (Fictitious character)—Fiction.   2. English
     teachers—Texas—Fiction.   I. Title.
          PS3553.R497D3   1994
          813'.54—dc20   93-42591
                              CIP

Printed in the United States of America
2 4 6 8 10 9 7 5 3 1

To Clare Scherz

A little learning is a dangerous thing;
Drink deep, or taste not the Pierian spring.

—Alexander Pope,
"An Essay on Criticism"

. . . A Dangerous Thing

$\triangledown$

1

CARL BURNS KNEW that the new dean wasn't going to work out when she bought the goat.

Her neighbors were outraged, but Burns had to admit that in theory, as the dean explained, having a goat running loose in the yard was a pretty good idea. That way, you never had to mow the grass, thus saving time for scholarship and study, saving gasoline or electricity that might have been used for a power mower, and at the same time providing the lawn with a generous portion of natural fertilizer.

Goats also dispensed a very healthy milk, from which an equally healthy cheese could be made, or so Burns had been informed, not that he cared to find out personally whether it was true or not. Though he had been quite fond of *Heidi* as a child, the phrase "goat cheese," no matter how much it might appeal to the yuppified tastes of the nation in general, made Burns think of something dark and smelly and awful, maybe containing short, coarse hairs.

Besides the milk and cheese, another argument in favor of goats was that they were, if you did not become too attached to them, quite good when barbecued. Burns had actually tried *cabrito* more than once, and it wasn't bad, except for the occasional presence of the short, coarse hairs that he dreaded finding in the cheese. They weren't very appetizing in barbecue, either.

As far as anyone in Pecan City could discover, however, there were no ordinances against keeping animals within the city limits. There were a number of people in town who had a few chickens. One man even had a horse in his backyard.

Of course, none of *those* people happened to be the academic dean at Hartley Gorman College.

"Thank God, I wasn't on the selection committee," Mal Tomlin said, tilting back his chair and puffing on his Merit Menthol 100. "No one can blame me for this one."

"There's nothing wrong with goats," Earl Fox said.

He *had* been on the selection committee and was therefore regarded by Burns and Tomlin as at least partially responsible for the choice of Dr. Gwendolyn Partridge as HGC's new academic dean.

Fox lit up a Merit he had mooched from Tomlin and blew a defiant plume of smoke at the sign affixed to the wall of the history department lounge. The sign was composed of white letters on a black background and had once read

NO SMOKING
PUBLIC AREA

Someone with a felt-tip marker, most likely one of the three men in the room, though none of them would ever have admitted it, had altered the sign by blacking out some of the white letters so that it now appeared to read

SMOKING
PUB IC AREA

"No one said there was anything wrong with goats," Burns said. "It's the other things." Burns was chairman of HGC's English department, and some of the "other things" had him much more worried than did the new dean's goat.

"She's one of those unreconstructed hippies," Tomlin said. He was worried too. "Those people never know when to let well enough alone."

Tomlin was especially bitter because one of Dr. Partridge's first decrees had been that as of March 1, all HGC buildings would become "smoke-free areas." It was bad enough that Tomlin, Fox, and Burns, who had himself quit smoking anyhow, were no longer supposed to smoke in the department lounge; now they weren't going to be allowed to smoke anywhere except outside.

Defying the rule in the lounge was easy enough, since only the three of them ever used the room and so far no one had seen fit to enforce the edict. The new rule, however, meant that someone was going to be cracking down.

Fox was bitter, too. He enjoyed smoking, but he went to great lengths to conceal from the students and administration the fact that he did so. While the habit wasn't exactly forbidden on campus at present, it certainly wasn't encouraged, and Fox did not want anyone to catch him in the act. If he was forced outside, he wasn't sure he could find a place to hide.

"Besides," Tomlin said, "everyone knows that Burns should have been the new dean."

Fox brushed ashes off the front of his shirt, a hideous, predominately green paisley job with puffy sleeves and a collar with at least seven-inch points. He'd paid a quarter for it at a garage sale, and he didn't want anything to happen to it.

An alligator-shaped ashtray sat in the middle of the rickety card table that was the only furniture in the small room, aside from the equally rickety chairs, and Fox tapped his cigarette on the alligator's side to remove the remaining ash.

"Burns didn't want to be dean," Fox said, looking at his shirt front again to be sure he hadn't set himself on fire. "He was invited to apply, you remember."

Both Fox and Tomlin stared at Burns, who wished he were somewhere else.

"It's not my fault you don't like the new dean," he said.

"It's your fault you didn't apply," Tomlin said, waving a hand and trailing a plume of smoke through the air. "You could have saved us from all this."

"Sorry about that," Burns said, though he really wasn't and, though no matter how they tried, his colleagues could not make him feel the least bit guilty.

Burns had no desire to be a dean. As a department chair,

he was still pretty much in control of his own life. He could leave his office and go to the library if he felt like it, or just walk around the campus, or even go to get a haircut. He could go home whenever he wanted to, within reason, but deans were eight-to-fivers, forced to remain behind a desk most of the day, writing reports and waiting for the phone to ring. If they did get to leave their offices, it was usually to attend another in an endless series of brain-numbing committee meetings.

Besides, Burns still enjoyed the classroom too much to want to move into administration. When Franklin Miller, HGC's new president, had invited Burns to apply for the open position, he had steadfastly refused to do so.

Fox crushed out his cigarette in the hollow of the alligator's back. "It just goes to show what happens when you believe letters of recommendation," he said.

As a matter of fact, Dr. Gwendolyn Partridge had come very highly recommended indeed. Her former employers had praised her intelligence, her diligence, her leadership abilities, her character, her scholarship, her meticulous attention to detail, and her ability to get along well with others.

"They didn't mention the goat, though, did they?" Tomlin said, looking up at the naked bulb that hung down above the card table. The bulb was wreathed in smoke.

"There were quite a few things they didn't mention," Fox said.

They hadn't mentioned, for example, that Dr. Partridge was quite liberal, at least as people living in Pecan City and connected with HGC understood the term. She was, in fact, an openly avowed feminist, and that was one source of the problems that were beginning to afflict Carl Burns.

Another source was Eric Holt, a new faculty member in the English department, one whom Dr. Partridge had insisted on hiring.

"There is no real research scholarship being undertaken by anyone in your area, is there, Dr. Burns?" Partridge had asked at their first meeting.

She might not have been the unreconstructed hippie Tomlin thought she was, but she was certainly the right age to have been a member of the counterculture of the early seventies. She still wore her dark brown hair straight and longer than shoulder length, and she made no attempt to hide the fact that there were now many more gray streaks in it than there had once been. She wore no makeup to cover the wrinkles at the corners of her eyes and mouth. She wore rimless glasses and had piercing black eyes. Burns was not in the least tempted to lie to her.

"No," he said. "There's not really much scholarly research going on." By which he meant there was none at all.

Of course the fact that HGC faculty members taught a fifteen-hour course load each semester had a lot to do with the lack of research. No one really expected an instructor to grade upward of 400 freshman themes a semester, in addition to preparing for classes, sponsoring clubs, and being involved in school activities, while at the same time doing deep scholarly research and producing papers with titles like "Male and Female: Androgyny in the 'Nancy Drew' Series."

"That's why I'm bringing in Dr. Holt," Partridge said. "He's quite a well-known critic and scholar, as you must know, and I'm sure he'll add a great deal of prestige to your department. You can use another teacher, I'm sure."

Burns had to agree. Enrollment, which had sunk to an all-time low under the auspices of HGC's former dean and president, both now departed, had increased already under Franklin Miller's guidance, and another instructor in the English department would be welcome. So Holt had come on board right after the end of the fall semester, along with Dr. Partridge.

The first trouble arose when Holt was assigned only three classes, at Dr. Partridge's insistence.

"We can't expect him to do his writing and research if he's overloaded with classroom time," Dr. Partridge said, to which the rest of the English faculty responded in unison,

"Why not let us have some release time? Then we'll do research, too."

Even Miss Darling joined in the protest, though she was on the brink of retirement and so far as Burns knew had not done any research since the day she'd completed her master's thesis on Sidney Lanier, nearly fifty years earlier.

Dr. Partridge's answer to the instructors' protests was simple. "Dr. Holt is an established scholar. We know the caliber of work that he can be expected to produce. You, on the other hand, are unknowns. If you produce some work and prove your capabilities, then we'll see about a reduction in teaching load."

Since it was virtually impossible to do any research without a reduction in load, Dr. Partridge's answer was a perfect catch-22 solution that made no one happy, except possibly Holt. There were many dark whisperings about the supposed relationship between the new dean and the new English teacher, though as far as anyone had been able to find out for sure there was no relationship at all. They had never even been employed at the same school.

Some of the faculty even suspected that Holt was Partridge's hatchet man and that Carl Burns was soon going to be history. Burns knew that such a possibility was not entirely farfetched. There was an old joke about how department chairmen were like mushrooms: You keep them in the dark, pile shit on them, and then you can them.

As far as Mal Tomlin was concerned, Holt, like Partridge, was just another old hippie. "And that's why you better watch your butt," he warned Burns. "They stick together, and you're not politically correct. That's your trouble. Yours, too, Fox."

That was another problem, all right. The curriculum in both the English and history departments left a lot to be desired as far as the new dean and her handpicked professor were concerned.

"The same old Euro-centered bull," was the way Eric Holt

put it as he looked over the textbooks that Burns gave him on Holt's first visit to the campus, the week before spring semester classes began. "DWEMs."

"Excuse me?" Burns said, though he knew very well what Holt meant.

"Euro-centered bull. The same old Dead White European Male writers that have been crammed down students' throats for thousands of years. Homer. Virgil. Dante. Chaucer. Shakespeare. Milton. Pope. Wordsworth. Keats," Holt said, slamming the heavy literature book shut. "What your department needs, Burns, is some new texts."

Naturally he didn't say "books." People like Holt didn't talk about "books." They talked about "texts."

Burns and Holt were meeting in Burns's office in Main, a place that Burns usually found quite pleasant. It had been built in what he suspected was an elevator shaft on the side of Main, and so it had windows looking out on the campus from three sides.

Some people wouldn't have considered the campus much to look at in January, but Burns liked the bare branches of the huge pecan trees, the crisp brown grass, the leafless vines that straggled up Main's stone walls. The place had a certain bleak grandeur, and Main in winter had always reminded Burns of the House of Usher.

Holt had a certain grandeur of his own, and it was far from bleak. He had a large head with a thick, dark beard; Burns had no doubt that he would set many young women's pulses aflutter. He was tall and imperially slim, dressed in a dark blue wool-blend suit with a double-breasted jacket. Burns thought that he probably glittered when he walked.

Holt also had an interesting history. Unlike most—or all, as far as Burns knew—well-known scholars, Holt had never worked at a major university. He had taught for most of his career at one small backwater school, not much different from HGC. His articles were published in the best journals, but he chose never to read papers at scholarly meetings. With his scholarly reputation, he had beyond question received numerous offers to teach at major universities, but he had never accepted any of them.

He seemed to enjoy casting himself as a learned hermit who liked to hole up in a small academic community and not be burdened with the distractions of a major university—distractions like committee meetings, pedagogical controversies, and departmental politics, all of which he could be insulated from at a small school with a friendly dean on his side. But he didn't want to grow stagnant, or so he said; therefore he had welcomed the change to another small college.

"What new material would you suggest?" Burns asked, though he had a pretty good idea what the answer would be. He had read several of Holt's articles.

"Anything but this," Holt said, laying the book on Burns's desk. "Anything but the tired old canon of tired old writers."

"We're in a sort of special situation here at Hartley Gorman College," Burns said. He had never thought he would find himself in the position of having to defend Shakespeare as part of the curriculum, but that was what it amounted to. "Our students come from mostly rural areas, and they aren't particularly well read. We've always felt that it was our job to give them a little taste of some of the works that are part of their cultural heritage."

"There you go," Holt said. He leaned back in the uncomfortable chair that Burns had provided him, perfectly at ease, almost smug. "Did you hear what you said? 'Their cultural heritage.' But it isn't, you see."

"Of course it is," Burns said, wishing that he felt as comfortable in the conversation as Holt appeared to be.

"No it isn't," Holt said. "You have quite a few people of color enrolled here. A number of Mexican-Americans. A few African-Americans and Asians. These works aren't *their* heritage."

Burns wanted to argue that all the students Holt had mentioned, with the probable exception of the Asians, were probably at least second-generation U. S. residents, and that the works in the text were as relevant to them as they were to anyone at the school.

But he didn't. He said, "So you're suggesting that we substitute other works, even if they haven't been proved to be of lasting significance?"

Holt didn't sneer. Not quite. He said, "You've heard of deconstructionist theory, I hope?"

"Yes," Burns said, experiencing a sinking feeling. "I guess you're going to tell me that what it boils down to is that you can't really say that one literary work is superior to another."

"Very good," Holt said. "So let's give these students something they need and want. For your traditional students, there are Louis L'Amour and Sue Grafton. For the others, there are books by Black Elk, Alice Walker, N. Scott Momaday, Thomas Sanchez. And you need many more works by women. Alice Munro. Joyce Carol Oates. Bobbie Ann Mason. Amy Tan."

Burns had nothing against any of those writers—in fact, he had read and enjoyed all of them. But he thought that students might read them on their own, outside of class, and that a foundation in the more traditionally accepted classics might be in order in a college curriculum.

"Multiculturalism, Burns, that's the key," Holt said. "You're too white-bread."

"Don't blame me," Burns said. "Blame my heredity and environment."

Holt laughed. At least he had a sense of humor. Burns went on to say that he thought the HGC curriculum did teach about other cultures: the cultures of the ancient Greeks, the ancient Romans, and the Italians of the Renaissance, to name a few.

Holt didn't agree, and neither did Dean Partridge. Those cultures might have been different, but they weren't the correct ones. So when the semester began, Holt was teaching three sections of a "special studies" survey of literature. The enrollment was small, but Holt and Partridge were sure it would grow as soon as other students found out about it.

Burns was sure the enrollment would grow, too. In addition to teaching a sort of "lit lite" course, Holt required no papers and gave no tests.

"What really matters is the reader's response to the readings," he said. "I grade very heavily on class participation."

"I see," Burns said, wondering when the smoldering resentment among the rest of his faculty members would burst into open rebellion.

Bunni, Burns's student secretary, was taking one of Holt's classes, and she talked to Burns about it one day.

"That Dr. Holt is really smart," she said. "I never realized how oppressed we women were until he explained things to us."

George (The Ghost) Kaspar, Bunni's boyfriend, was with her. He didn't look especially happy with what Bunni was discovering about oppression.

"Have you been oppressing Bunni?" Burns asked him.

"No," George said. "Or at least I don't think so. But Dr. Holt says I've been oppressing lots of other people."

"Who?" Burns asked, genuinely curious. He would not have guessed that George was the type to oppress anyone.

"Well," George said, looking at the worn grayish-green carpet that covered the floor, "gays."

Burns hadn't known there were any homosexuals at HGC, and he wondered how George had found the opportunity to oppress any. So he asked.

"That's just it," George said. "See? You're doing it, too."

"I am?" Burns said. "How?"

"By assuming that everyone else is straight just because you are. When you do that, you oppress others."

"Oh," Burns said, mentally bracing himself for the student and parent complaints that were sure to come as a result of such radical ideas being spread across the HGC campus.

His only comfort, and it was small comfort indeed, was that Earl Fox was being threatened with a new faculty member of his own for the fall semester.

"It seems that we don't teach history properly," Fox said, jabbing the air with another of Tomlin's Merits.

Little puffs of smoke came off the end of the cigarette with each jab and floated toward the light. Fox had once burned a hole in the headliner of his car jabbing a cigarette like that. He had told his wife that Mal Tomlin did it.

"We have entirely the wrong perspective on things," Fox went on. "There's not enough in the text we use about white men's vile treatment of the Native Americans or the Puritans' rape of the New England environment. And that's just for starters."

"Hippies," Tomlin said darkly. As chairman of the education department, he would be the next one threatened. "I think we ought to find out a little more about Partridge and Holt. What do we really know about them, after all? Did anybody call the schools where they came from to find out what was behind those good letters of recommendation?"

"President Miller did," Fox said. "Nobody had anything but good to say about Dr. Partridge."

"Well, they wouldn't," Tomlin said. "Probably glad to be rid of her."

Fox took a drag of the Merit and said, "Tom Henderson told me the other day that he thought Holt looked familiar. Thought he might have known him. You think that's possible?"

Henderson taught sociology and psychology. He had been at HGC for a long time, having come there directly from graduate school.

"They're about the same age," Burns said. "But I don't know when Henderson would have known him. And I don't see what difference it makes."

"There's something going on," Tomlin said. "Has to be. Why else would Partridge bring him here? Those two knew each other somehow. You can count on it. I think you ought to talk to Henderson, Burns, see what you can find out."

"Why me?" Burns said.

"Because you're the one who can find things out," Tomlin

said. "Whenever there's a mystery, we can count on you."

"He's right," Fox said. "Even the chief of police knows how good you are at solving things."

Burns wasn't so sure that Boss Napier, chief of the Pecan City police department, would have agreed with that statement, but he could see that it wouldn't do any good to argue.

"All right," he said. "I'll talk to Henderson, but I don't expect anything to come of it."

"If it doesn't, we still have hope," Tomlin said. "Holt is tied to the new dean, and she'll never last, not if she keeps that goat."

"Right," Fox said. "So maybe we'd better just leave well enough alone. You know what happened the last time Burns got involved with a dean."

"Aw, come on," Tomlin said. "This could never be like that. After all, what are the odds of two deans getting murdered at a college as small as this one?"

"You're right," Fox said. "I was just trying to make a little joke."

"Well, it wasn't a very good one," Tomlin said. "Look at Burns. He's turned pale as a ghost."

"Must be the smoke getting to me," Burns said, waving a hand in front of his face.

"That's what you get for quitting," Tomlin said.

Burns smiled weakly, but he knew the smoke wasn't really the problem. For some strange reason, he'd felt a sudden chill when Tomlin had mentioned murder.

It's a good thing I don't believe in premonitions, he thought. Then the bell rang, and he forgot all about it.

2

Burns, Fox, and Tomlin had been taking their usual break while the students were in Assembly, which had been known as Chapel until the majority of programs started featuring country-and-western musicians and secular speakers and therefore became too worldly for its original title in the judgment of HGC officials. Few faculty members attended, preferring instead to use the time for grading or, as in the case of Burns and his friends, relaxing.

Tomlin and Fox both had classes immediately after Assembly, but Burns did not. He walked back upstairs to his office, which was directly above the history department lounge, to grade some of the papers from his remedial writing class.

Not that it was called a remedial class. At least the English department was politically correct to that degree. It would never do to tell a group of entering college freshmen that they were writing on approximately the third-grade level. The course was instead called "developmental writing."

Reading the papers was infinitely depressing work, and Burns vowed that if he ever taught the course again he would never assign a topic like "My Goals for the Future."

He knew that he should never—*would* never—tell his students that their goals were unattainable. He didn't want to discourage them, and besides, that was another politically incorrect idea. All students were supposed to be capable of becoming anything they wanted to become, no matter what their apparent limitations.

He looked at the first sentence of the paper he was holding, written in a nearly illegible scrawl by one Randy Randall: "Im goin too get my english grad up wile Im hear at Hortley Groman Collage and wen I get it up Im goin too majer in goverment, then Im goin too be a lowyer, have lots of money, nice car like a Mursades a big house and etc."

Burns sighed. Okay, so it was early in the semester. Only three weeks gone so far, twelve to go. But just how realistic was it to think that he could help a student like Randy Randall raise his writing ability to anywhere near the level he would need to succeed in a regular undergraduate class, much less in law school? Maybe if he had fifteen years rather than fifteen weeks, he could do something, but would even that be enough?

Burns laid the paper on his desk. Maybe Eric Holt was right, though for the wrong reasons. Maybe it was pointless to try teaching Shakespeare to classes full of people who were only marginally better writers than Randy Randall. Maybe Louis L'Amour *was* more appropriate.

Burns took the second paper, by Tammi Sliger, from the stack and started reading. "My goal is to get out of this dumb class and into a real class I don't belong in this class I always made good grades in high school I am real good in English."

Burns wondered where Tammi had gone to high school, but at least she could spell, even if she didn't have a particularly good grasp of proper sentence structure. Or maybe it was simply punctuation she didn't understand. If she paid any attention at all in class, she might actually learn enough to help her write a passable paper.

The "if" was what bothered Burns. There was more than one student in the developmental class who seemed to regard being there as more of a punishment than an opportunity to learn anything. Those students retained the same bad habits that had doomed them to a developmental class in the first place. They stared out the windows, doodled in their notebooks, worked on their math assignments, even put their heads down and slept, openmouthed and drooling, on their desks. Burns heard one of the latter explain his drowsiness to a friend as they were leaving class one day: "Hey, I was up till four o'clock playing Nintendo. I was lucky to get here at all."

Burns wondered briefly if maybe he should have gone into administration after all. He shoved the papers aside and stood up. He needed a break. He thought it might be a good idea to go to the library.

He wasn't going to check out a book. He was going to check out the librarian.

In his estimation, one of the best things that had happened to Hartley Gorman College in years was Elaine Tanner, the new librarian, who had arrived at the beginning of the fall semester. She was quite pretty, with honey-colored hair and green eyes. And she spent her time dealing with books. What more could an English teacher ask for?

As Burns descended the stairway in Main, he looked down at the worn and frayed carpet that covered the steps. There were places where it was worn through to the pad, and now even the pad was disintegrating. Burns remembered when the carpet had been new; this thought vaguely depressed him, so he pushed it aside. Maybe now that enrollment was on the rise, the carpet would be replaced. He hoped so.

He pushed open the doors on the east side of the building and went out. The sky was infinitely blue, and the sun threw crisp shadows on the brown grass, giving the day a springlike appearance that was seriously misleading. The temperature was in the low thirties, and the wind was swooshing straight down from the polar ice cap. It lifted Burns's short brown hair and flapped the tails of his wool sport coat.

When he got to the library, the building blocked off most of the wind, and he paused for a moment to reflect on his pleasure that Dr. Partridge had abandoned the practice of referring to all the campus buildings by number. Formerly, the library had been Hartley Gorman III and had to be given its proper title in all memos and documents. Burns had hated the rule, and he was glad to see that Dr. Partridge seemed to think it was silly, too.

He entered the building through the E.R. Memorial doors and went past the circulation desk to Elaine's office. She was there, surrounded by trophies of all kinds.

There was a trophy for finishing in first place in the Pecan City Fun Run in 1979. There was a trophy for "Prize Bull" in the 1968 Youth Fair. There was one for baking, and there were several for baton twirling. There was one from a bowling league, and one from a chili cook-off. There was even one for catching the big bass in a fishing tournament.

There were short trophies and tall ones. There were trophies sitting on bases of fake marble and trophies with elaborate stands of red, white, and blue. There were trophies surmounted by statuettes of Winged Victory and trophies topped by straining sprinters.

There were trophies on the desk, on the bookshelves, and on the floor.

Anyone entering the office would get the idea that Elaine Tanner was a woman of many accomplishments, and that might even be true. But the fact was that she had earned none of the trophies herself.

She had bought them at flea markets, thrift shops, and garage sales.

As she explained it to Burns, she bought them because being surrounded by symbols of accomplishment increased her self-esteem. And she didn't tell just everyone that she hadn't won the trophies herself.

Burns couldn't understand why a woman as good-looking as Elaine Tanner would need to increase her self-esteem, unless it had something to do with those big round glasses she wore, which as far as Burns was concerned simply emphasized her eyes and didn't make her one bit less attractive. But if she wanted to buy trophies, there was nothing wrong with that. It seemed like a harmless enough eccentricity.

"Good morning," she said when he came through her open door. She had a low, husky voice that always made Burns's stomach flutter. "And how's your semester going?"

Burns moved a calf-roping trophy out of a chair and sat down. "Not so well," he said. He brought her up to date on his discussion with Fox and Tomlin.

She did not seem especially concerned. "There's nothing wrong with being politically correct," she said when he was finished. "This place could do with a little more of that sort of thing."

Burns ran a hand through his hair, hoping that it would lie flat. "For example?" he asked.

"All right. Let's start with you. Do you think of yourself as a department chair*man*?"

"Uh-oh," Burns said. Of course he did. For that matter, he thought of Faye Smith of the math and science department as a chairman, even though she was definitely a woman. True, she wore cowboy boots, jeans, and western shirts to teach in, but there was no mistaking her sex.

"And I've noticed your use of pronouns, too," Elaine said. "You say things like 'The student left *his* book in the car.' "

That was true. Burns had to admit it. He found saying something like 'The student left his or her book in the car' awkward and silly. Of course you could get out of situations like that by rephrasing the sentence, but who had time to think of rephrasing sentences in the course of ordinary conversation?

"And another thing," Elaine went on. "You—"

"Never mind," Burns said, holding up a hand. "I get the idea. And you're right. I'll try to reform, but don't expect me to spell women 'w-o-m-y-n.' Or to say that Earl Fox teaches 'herstory.' "

Elaine laughed. "All right, I won't. Now what else is bothering you?"

"Is it that obvious?" Burns asked. He told her about the papers he had been reading.

"That's more serious," she said. She looked around her office, as if thinking about giving Burns one of her trophies. Or maybe she was thinking about giving them to his students.

"It's not that they're stupid, either," Burns said. "I'm sure that some of them, maybe most of them, are quite good at any number of things."

"But not writing," Elaine said.

"Definitely not writing."

"Do you encourage them, give them lots of positive feedback?"

Burns was usually suspicious of phrases like "positive feedback," but not when Elaine used them. "Sure I do," he said. "I try to be as positive as possible."

For some reason, one of Mal Tomlin's favorite stories popped into his mind; the punch line was, "For a fat woman, you sure don't sweat much." Burns supposed you couldn't joke about fat people anymore. "Calorically challenged," maybe.

"Well, I know you're a good teacher, so that can't be the problem," Elaine said.

She didn't really have any way to judge how good a teacher he was, but Burns appreciated the compliment anyway.

"I don't know," he said. "Sometimes I don't think I'm doing such a good job. Maybe I should have considered taking the dean's position."

Elaine shook her head. "You wouldn't have been happy. If you want to do something else, maybe you should get into police work. Ever since you caught that shoplifter last Christmas, R.M. says that you might have investigative abilities."

"R.M." was Pecan City's police chief, Boss Napier, and it really bothered Burns to hear Elaine refer to him so familiarly. He would never, even in his wildest imaginings, have thought that he and Napier would become romantic rivals, but that was exactly what had happened, and Elaine seemed to take what Burns deemed was an unseemly amount of pleasure in stringing both men along.

"I'd make a lousy policeman—"

"Police*man*?"

"Police*person*, then," Burns said. He thought the word

was absurd, but he was weak in Elaine's presence. "Whatever you call them, I'd be terrible. I may have to take it under consideration, though." He told her about the suspicion some people had voiced about Eric Holt being groomed to take over Burns's job.

"That's ridiculous," Elaine said, reaching out and brushing a speck of dust off one of her bowling trophies. "Why would Dr. Partridge do something like that?"

"Who knows?" Burns said. "There's no rule that says deans have to have reasons that anyone else would understand."

"Don't be so gloomy. You always look on the dark side of things. Why don't you do something positive, instead?"

"Like what?"

"I don't know. You're the person with investigative abilities, not me."

"There's nothing to investigate," Burns said.

"If there are rumors, there's something to investigate. Rumors don't just start from nothing."

Burns found himself smiling. "Around here, they do."

And that was true. There were always rumors of one kind or another swirling around at Hartley Gorman College. Gossip was one of the most popular pastimes at the school, but then Burns supposed it was a popular pastime in almost any organization of any size.

"Maybe I could find out a little something about Holt, though," he said, remembering what Fox had mentioned about Tom Henderson.

"What kind of something?" Elaine asked.

Burns didn't know. Even Henderson hadn't seemed too definite in his comment to Fox. Still, the whole business of Holt's coming to HGC so suddenly seemed very suspicious.

Gwendolyn Partridge had a degree in literature, and she had no doubt read Holt's articles in the journals, but why would the idea of having Holt come to Hartley Gorman ever occur to her in the first place? Wasn't it more than likely that there *was* some connection between them, just as some of the rumors implied?

And why would Holt come to Hartley Gorman, for God's sake? Sure, he was already teaching in a community no larger than Pecan City and at a college that probably had a library no better than the one at HGC, but he was established where he was. Why change just because he was asked?

"I think I'll talk to a few people," Burns said, getting out of the chair.

He picked up the calf-roping trophy to replace it, but Elaine stopped him.

"Just leave that on the floor. I found it at a garage sale last weekend, and I haven't made a place for it on the shelves yet."

"You didn't happen to see Earl Fox at the sale, did you?" Burns asked.

"As a matter of fact, I did. He was buying some polyester pants."

Burns nodded. It figured.

"That new Kevin Costner movie starts Friday night," he said, changing the subject. "Would you like to go?"

Elaine looked at a trophy on the front of her desk. It was topped by a strutting twirler made of gold plastic.

"R.M. mentioned something about a basketball game," she said finally.

Burns was not surprised. Napier, though he didn't look the part, had proved to be a regular Casanova.

"You could come with us," Elaine said. "I'm sure R.M. wouldn't mind."

"Ha," Burns said.

Elaine turned her big green eyes on him. "Now, just what is that supposed to mean?"

"What?"

"That noise you made. That 'ha' sound. What is that supposed to mean?"

"It's supposed to mean 'ha,' " Burns said.

"I don't know why you don't try a little harder to get along with R.M.," Elaine said.

"Ha," Burns said again.

It wasn't that he and Napier didn't get along, exactly. Their relationship was never going to rival that of Aeneas and faithful Achates, but they did get along. Or at least they got along when Elaine Tanner wasn't part of the equation.

Burns liked to think he had the advantage with Elaine because of propinquity, if nothing else, but he was beginning to wonder.

"Maybe I'll see you at the game," he said.

3

THE COUNSELING OFFICE at Hartley Gorman College was located on the first floor of Main (Hartley Gorman I in the old system that Burns was trying to forget, obviously without too much success so far). It shared quarters with the records office, and both of them were crammed in among the offices of the education department and the print shop.

The counselors had a difficult job. They had to advise students about which courses to take, explain which courses would transfer to other schools and which courses HGC accepted in transfer, deal with students who had learning difficulties, handle violations of the student behavior code, help students with their degree plans, and interpret the arcane secrets of the HGC catalog for students who could not figure them out for themselves. They also handled admissions testing and were responsible for placing students in the correct courses after their enrollment.

Or those were some of the things they were *supposed* to do. Burns was not sure just how many of them were actually accomplished, or accomplished with any degree of efficiency.

One reason for his doubts was that he received calls semester after semester asking the same question: "Can students take British literature before American literature, or does it make any difference?"

It wasn't the question itself that bothered him. What bothered him was that the same counselor called him to ask it over and over. Maybe even that wouldn't have been so bad if the answer to the question were not printed in the catalog for anyone to see and read. The counselors were supposed to be the college's experts on the catalog, weren't they? Burns could not avoid the nagging worry that if they were, then the college was in big trouble.

When he entered the office, he was greeted by Dawn Melling, the very one who could never seem to get the course sequences straight. She was a statuesque young woman with a large bust, a small waist, and long red fingernails. She had a huge beehive of dark black hair that Burns was certain was a wig, though why anyone would choose such a wig he wasn't quite sure. She looked a little like Elvira, except that her dress wasn't as revealing as those usually chosen by the Mistress of the Dark.

"Why, Dr. Burns," she said. "What brings you here?" She was from Georgia and had a pronounced Southern drawl, though she had not lived in Georgia since she had come to HGC as a student ten years previously.

"I, uh, want to look at some catalogs," Burns said.

Being around Dawn always disturbed him. Her overtly sexy appearance had something to do with it, but she was by all accounts happily married to Walt Melling, the school's chief recruiter, and Burns was sure she would never dream of straying. What disturbed him was a certain vagueness in her character, a certain je ne sais quoi that kept Burns off balance in every conversation they ever had.

In other words, he was never quite sure what she was talking about. Once he had seen her in the parking lot, getting out of a brand new Ford Taurus, and he asked her how she liked the new car.

She reached into the car and retrieved her briefcase, then turned to Burns. "Drives like a glove," she said.

Burns never had figured out just what she meant, though it wasn't for want of trying. Sometimes he would wake up from a deep sleep and think, " 'Drives like a glove'?"

"Which catalogs are you looking for?" she asked now.

"College catalogs," Burns said, so she wouldn't give him the latest from J. C. Penney. "From *other* colleges," he added,

so that she wouldn't give him a handful of HGC catalogs
and shoo him out.

"Of course you do," she said. "Right this way."

She turned and led him into a small cubbyhole beside the
main office. On one wall there was a shelf filled with
paperbound catalogs of all shapes and sizes.

"Were you looking for anything in particular?" Dawn
asked. She sounded like a salesclerk in the clothing department at Sears.

"I think I can find it," Burns said. He didn't want anyone
looking over his shoulder while he searched.

"Just call me if you need any help," Dawn said. "I know
all about these things." She waved a red-tipped hand at the
crammed shelves.

"Thanks," Burns said, convinced that she knew absolutely nothing at all about the contents of the catalogs.

He waited until she had left the room before he looked for
the one he wanted. Since they were arranged more or less in
alphabetical order, he found it easily and pulled it from the
shelf.

The spine was royal blue, as was most of the front cover,
and the words CATALOG OF AUSTAMONT COLLEGE were
printed on it in white.

Burns sat at the student desk that was the only piece of
furniture in the room and opened the catalog to the back.
He wasn't interested in the course descriptions. He was
interested in the list of faculty members. Austamont College
was one of HGC's sister denominational institutions, located in Missouri. It was the school where Gwendolyn
Partridge had been before her recent move, and hers was the
first name Burns looked for.

It was there, all right:

PARTRIDGE, GWENDOLYN E. *Professor of English. Chair,
Division of Language and Literature. B.A., M.A., Ph.D., Texas
Tech University. 1977.*

That year was the date that Dr. Partridge had joined the
faculty at Austamont, and it was probably also the year she

had received her final degree. She had become a division chair at Austamont; the next step up the ladder was a deanship, which had apparently not become available to her at that school, for whatever reason. So she had applied for the one at HGC.

Burns then scanned the list of faculty members for the name of someone he might know, either from graduate school or professional meetings.

Only one name was even slightly familiar, that of Barry Towson. Burns had talked to him about paperback mystery fiction at a meeting of the Popular Culture Association in San Antonio the previous year. They had agreed on a fondness for writers not generally much remembered by the general public, writers like J. M. Flynn, Bob McKnight, and Milton K. Ozaki. Towson would probably remember him, Burns thought.

Burns flipped back to the beginning of the catalog and copied down the school's area code and phone number.

Then he replaced the catalog and took down the one from Claireson University, where Holt had taught before arriving at HGC. Flipping to the faculty listing, Burns noted that Holt's degrees were from North Texas State University (now for some reason known as The University of North Texas).

That was funny, Burns thought. Mal Tomlin was about Holt's age, and Tomlin's degrees were from North Texas. Yet, as far as Burns knew, Tomlin had never mentioned having encountered Holt there. Of course, in the seventies there had probably been a large number of students in pursuit of graduate degrees in English there, and Tomlin was in another department entirely, so there was nothing unusual in the fact that their paths had never crossed.

Burns looked through the faculty listing for other names he might recognize, but this time he came up with none. Well, he could ask Tomlin to call a few of his friends from graduate school to see if they had known Holt, and there was always Tom Henderson, who thought Holt looked familiar.

Burns returned the catalog to the shelf and left the cubbyhole.

"Did you find what you were looking for?" Dawn Melling asked as he emerged.

"Yes," Burns said. "Thanks, Dawn."

She smiled, revealing startlingly white teeth. "Anytime. Come back and let us service you again."

Pondering the implications of that last statement, Burns left the counseling office and headed for the stairs.

Tom Henderson's office was on the second floor of Main, on the opposite side of the building from Earl Fox's. The location was a matter of the building's structure and was not a deliberate gesture on Fox's part, though the truth of the matter was that Henderson was a burr under Fox's saddle, a more or less constant source of irritation. Burns did not wish Fox any ill, but at the same time he was glad Henderson taught in Fox's department.

Henderson was a scrawny scarecrow of a man, the ninety-eight-pound weakling grown middle-aged. He felt threatened by anyone who dared question his absolute authority in the classroom, or who even *appeared* to question that authority.

Let a student wonder why he had received an 86 on a quiz while someone with identical answers had received an 87, and Henderson was likely to burst into a rage that purpled his leathery face and bulged his eyes.

And in this case, it was correct to use the masculine pronoun to refer to the student, because it was extremely rare for a female student in one of Henderson's classes to get anything but an excellent grade.

Burns had once overheard two women talking in the hall about Henderson's classes. One was recommending an introductory course to the other.

"Just be sure to wear a short skirt, sit in the front row, and cross your legs," the first one said. "You won't get any less than a B, I promise you."

Burns knew that Fox dealt with a number of complaints

every semester from students, generally males, who felt that Henderson had persecuted, teased, or tormented them; but so far there had been no complaints of sexual harassment. So far. Burns thought that maybe Henderson was one faculty member who could profit from a little political correctness.

Burns walked past the door of the men's room (and how politically correct was that appellation? he wondered), turned left, and went down the corridor to Henderson's office.

The door was closed, and Burns's first thought was that Henderson was in class. Then he heard muffled voices from behind the door and changed his mind.

He raised his hand to knock and almost hit a student in the forehead as the door was jerked open and she rushed out of the office.

She threw Burns a look and then swept by, but not before he saw the traces of tears on her cheeks.

He looked into the office. Henderson was standing by a window, hands in his pockets, looking out at the campus as if nothing untoward had occurred.

Maybe nothing had. Maybe the student had merely been upset by a homework assignment or a bad grade. It had happened before, even to Burns, who hoped that was all there was to this situation.

He tapped on the door jamb, and Henderson turned from the window.

"Hello, Burns," he said. He seemed perfectly calm. "Nice day, isn't it?"

"Too nice for anyone to be crying," Burns said.

Henderson smiled grimly. "Oh, that was nothing. She was just angry because she read the wrong assignment and therefore made a failing grade on one of my pop tests."

"Oh," Burns said. Incidents like that weren't uncommon. He thought about mentioning it to Fox later, however, just in case. "It happens."

"Too often," Henderson said. He sat behind his desk. It was much neater than Burns's own. There was nothing to be seen except a desk calendar and a bust of Sigmund Freud.

"Have a chair, Burns," Henderson said. "What can I do for you?"

Burns sat down and looked at Henderson, who was wearing a tan cardigan over an open-necked white shirt. There was a ruff of chest hair sticking out like the straw from a scarecrow's shirt. Burns wondered if Henderson let it show like that to compensate for the fact that he was a victim of male pattern baldness. Burns was reasonably sure that incipient baldness was the reason for Henderson's unfashionably long sideburns and the swirl of hair that hung over his collar in the back.

Or maybe I'm reading too much into things, Burns thought. Sit in an office with a bust of Freud, and there was no telling what strange thoughts would occur to you.

"I was wondering about Eric Holt," Burns said. "Earl says you mentioned something about his looking familiar."

Henderson opened the middle drawer of his desk and pulled out a pipe. He put the pipe in his mouth, but he didn't light it. "Getting ready for the smoke-free environment," he said by way of explanation. He gave the pipe a couple of dry puffs. "Not very satisfactory, though."

"Probably not," Burns said. "Have you remembered anything about Holt since you talked to Earl?"

"Not a thing," Henderson said. He took the pipe out of his mouth and laid it on the desk beside the bronze bust. "He looks familiar for some reason, but I can't put my finger on it."

"Maybe you knew him in grad school," Burns said. "He went to North Texas."

"It can't be that, then," Henderson said. "I went to school in California. San Diego State." He smiled. "I was certainly glad to get away from there. You can't imagine the things that went on there in those days."

Burns could imagine, all right, but that wasn't the point of his talking to Henderson. "Have you seen him at any professional meetings?"

"I don't know. Not unless he's been attending meetings

out of his field. I know that I haven't been going to any English meetings." He picked up the pipe again. "Is he in any trouble, Burns?"

"It's nothing," Burns said.

Henderson reached out bony fingers and fiddled with the pipe. "I've heard a few things," he said.

"Rumors," Burns said. He wasn't going to share anything with Henderson. "You know how things get started around this place."

Henderson's mouth twisted in a sort of grin. "Do I not."

Burns didn't have anything to say to that.

Henderson left off his fiddling with the pipe and leaned back in his chair, steepling his thin fingers and resting them against his pointy chin.

"I wouldn't be bothered by rumors if I were you, Burns," he said. "Too many good men are brought down by nothing more than the animosity spread by idle tongues."

Burns wondered if Henderson had been involved in some recent incident that Fox hadn't gotten around to telling him about. It wasn't likely. Henderson was no doubt speaking from past experience.

"You're probably right," Burns said. "I shouldn't let things like that bother me."

"True. But if you're really bothered, the best thing to do is to get things out in the open. Don't be afraid of a confrontation."

Henderson certainly wasn't afraid of confrontations. In fact, he seemed to encourage them. Burns, however, wasn't that sort of person. He glanced at Freud. There was probably some deep-seated reason in Burns's childhood that had caused him to be basically nonconfrontational, just as there was something in Henderson's that made him enjoy conflicts with others to the point that he actually sought them.

Burns stood up. "Thanks, Tom," he said. "You're right. I think I'll just do my job and not worry about everything I hear."

"I'm sure that's best," Henderson said.

Burns was sure, too, but that didn't mean he wasn't going to call Barry Towson.

It was almost noon, and Burns drove home to make the call. He could have called from his office and paid with his credit card, since it wasn't really a business call, but he didn't want the call to go through the school switchboard.

He was lucky and caught Towson in his office. The Austamont operator connected them.

Towson remembered Burns well, and he was eager to talk about unknown paperback writers. He was not, however, eager to talk about Gwendolyn Partridge and the great letters of recommendation that had been sent to Hartley Gorman College.

"You know how things are," Towson said.

"I'm not sure that I do," Burns said. "That's why I called you."

"You can't be too careful these days," Towson said.

Burns didn't get it. "About what?" he asked.

"About anything. Everything. You can't be too careful."

"I wish you'd help me out a little here, Barry. I don't know what you're trying to tell me."

There was a heavy sigh on the other end of the line. Then Towson said, "I'm trying to tell you that you have to be careful in everything you do. Even in writing letters of recommendation. When did you get your degree, Burns?"

Burns didn't know what that had to do with anything, but he told him.

"How were the letters of recommendation handled?"

Burns had to think about that for a second. It had been a while. Finally he remembered. "I got the professors to write the letters, and they sent them directly to the school's placement office," he said.

"And were you allowed to see the letters?" Towson asked.

"No," Burns said. "I went to the placement office to be sure all the letters were in my file, but I wasn't allowed to see them. Not even a glimpse."

"Things are nothing like that now," Towson said. "Letters are open to the person being recommended, and if he or she doesn't like what he or she sees, he or she can sue the pants off you."

Burns didn't think he'd ever heard so many "he or she's" in one sentence before. Dr. Partridge had undoubtedly been quite influential at Austamont.

"So what can you do?" he asked.

"If you write a letter, you make negatives into positives. A contentious person has 'a strong personality,' for example. A bully is 'a good leader.' You see what I mean?"

"Are you telling me that Dr. Partridge is a contentious bully?"

"I'm doing nothing of the sort." Towson's tone was resentful. "Don't put words into my mouth."

"But there were problems with Dr. Partridge?"

"I didn't say that."

"I know you didn't. I did, but—"

"Let's just say that Dr. Partridge was very strong-minded. That she wanted to make a lot of changes here at Austamont that a lot of people weren't ready for."

"Political correctness," Burns said.

"In a nutshell, yes," Towson said. "Not that many of the changes weren't for the better, mind you. Most of them, even. But in a small, conservative community—well, some of them just didn't sit too well."

"So no one was sorry to see Dr. Partridge go?"

"I didn't say that."

"Okay," Burns said. "You didn't say it. Let me ask you something easy. How did Dr. Partridge find out that there was an opening here at Hartley Gorman for an academic dean?"

There was a short silence. Towson cleared his throat and said, "I believe our president may have mentioned it to her. But I'm not certain about that."

Burns was. He could imagine the scene. Partridge goes into the president's office for a meeting or conference, and the talk turns to deanships. The president is sure she's administrative material, but there just never seem to be any openings at Austamont. However, the president has just noticed that there's a vacancy at good old Hartley Gorman College, "that fine little school down there in Texas. You're originally from Texas, aren't you, Dr. Partridge?" Her interest piqued, Dr. Partridge investigates, decides, with the blessings and strong recommendation of her president, to apply, and gets the job. HGC gets a new dean, and Austamont gets rid of potential controversy.

"Thanks, Barry," Burns said. "You've been a big help. By the way, do you know Eric Holt, by any chance?"

"Who?"

"Eric Holt. You must have seen his articles. He's published in things like *Modern Fiction Studies* and *The Journal of Popular Culture.*"

"Oh, sure. *That* Eric Holt. What about him?"

"Did he ever visit your campus, do a lecture there, anything like that?"

"No," Towson said. "Never. We don't get many visiting critics around here, especially not of Holt's caliber. Why do you ask?"

"He's working here now. I thought you might know him."

"I wish I did. It must be great to work with someone like that."

"Oh, it is," Burns lied. Then he changed the subject. "Now tell me. If you were making a list of the top ten paperback writers of the fifties and sixties, who'd be number one?"

That was a subject that Towson warmed to rapidly, and Burns, who had his own list, ran up quite a phone bill.

$\triangledown$

4

THAT WAS ALMOST the end of Burns's investigation, but then he decided that Tom Henderson had the right idea. The thing to do was to talk to Holt in person.

But first he looked over the list of paperback writers that Towson had come up with. Burns, who liked making lists, also liked comparing his lists with those others made, especially when the two did not necessarily agree. Towson ranked Harry Whittington at the top, for example, and Burns thought that was a good choice, depending on the criteria you used. Burns could never really make up his mind among Whittington, Jim Thompson, Charles Williams, and John D. MacDonald. You could certainly make a case for Donald Hamilton, too, though Hamilton hadn't really hit his stride until the early sixties.

Burns put the list in his desk and went back to school. It was nearly two o'clock, but there was no chance that he would miss Holt, who, unlike most members of the English department, liked afternoon classes. In fact, he taught one class on Mondays and Wednesdays from three until four thirty and another on Tuesdays and Thursdays from two thirty until four. His other class met on Tuesday evenings. That way he had most of the day open for his scholarly writing.

Burns parked his 1967 Plymouth on the street in front of Main and got out. The car looked like some kind of dinosaur among the Toyotas and Hondas and Ford Escorts. Because of the dry, cold air, Burns received a mild static shock when he shut the door.

When he mounted the front steps, he was faced by a note taped to the door.

PLEASE!
DO NOT WALK!!
ON WET FLOOR!!

Burns didn't want to get on the bad side of Rose. No matter what anyone said about who was in control of things, no matter how the organizational charts read, the secretaries and the maids were the really essential people at the school. A department chair could be gone for a week and no one would notice; if a secretary missed a day, there was chaos. And it would be easier to move the Rock of Gibraltar than to get a faculty member to empty a wastebasket. Some of them didn't even flush the toilet in the men's room.

Burns went around the building to the east entrance. He went inside and walked down the hallway to the front of the building, where he encountered the wet floor. The other floors and the stairways were carpeted, but the first floor retained its original hardwood covering.

Rose was at the other end of the front hall, jamming a yellow-handled mop up and down in a green plastic bucket and talking to herself, no doubt muttering about how she would deal with anyone who walked on her newly mopped floor. Burns thought she could do whatever she wanted to; she had broader shoulders than any member of the HGC football team.

He decided that he could evade her if he was careful and quiet. He tiptoed across the damp boards and catfooted it up the worn carpeting of the stairs without looking back.

He was out of breath when he reached the third floor, but that was only to be expected. The sixteen-foot ceilings of Main meant that there was quite a distance to cover between floors. Even the members of the track team were winded by their climb to their English classes, a fact that bothered Dr. Partridge.

She didn't really care about the track team, of course.

What bothered her was that Main was a quite politically incorrect building in that it posed formidable obstacles to the handicapped, which was a politically incorrect term, Burns knew, but he couldn't think of the right one. "Differently abled." That was it.

Because of the steps outside the building, it would be next to impossible for a person in, say, a wheelchair to get inside. If the person did get inside, the absence of an elevator meant that he (or she) would never be able to get above the first floor under his (or her) own power.

Burns had solved the problem on previous occasions in two different ways. One girl on crutches had been carried to the third floor by two football players, one of them carrying her from the first floor to the second, where the other took over and carried her the rest of the way. She hadn't weighed much, and Burns had convinced the football players that it was a good way to stay in shape during the off-season.

For wheelchair students, Burns had simply taught the required classes in the math building, which, being much newer, was equipped with ramps and elevators and was accessible to everyone.

Now Dr. Partridge wanted to make Main equally accessible. Rumor (and Burns believed this one) had it that Franklin Miller had turned ghostly pale when told the cost of an elevator. It could not be installed in the proposed shaft, which would have eliminated both Burns's office and the history lounge. It would have to be installed on the outside of the building. And no one was sure the outside would hold up to the stress that an elevator would place on it. The entire building would somehow have to be reinforced. So far the plan to build an elevator had therefore been stalled in Miller's office, though that would probably not be the end of things if Dr. Partridge had her way.

Burns stood at the top of the stair until he caught his breath, and then went to his office. There was no use talking to Holt now. It was nearly time for Holt's class to begin. The talk could wait until later. It was Tuesday, and since Burns and Holt both had evening classes, they could talk at four thirty.

Burns could spend the time until then grading his developmental papers. It wasn't a job he expected to enjoy.

. . . and then Ill play basketball for like the rockets or bulls make a buncha money then maybe make movies or be on tv, like a lot of ballplayers they go on tv and make money when they retire and get put up on a pedal-stool by there fans that's why Im am in radio and tv so Ill have a trade when I get out of sports except that if Im am in radio and tv I wont reely be out of sports for all intensive purposes but . . .

Burns put the paper down, laid his red pen down on top of it, and rubbed his eyes. If you looked at it in a certain way there was an almost Joycean quality to "put up on a pedal-stool" and "for all intensive purposes." It was too bad he couldn't look at it that way.

He looked up at the ceiling instead. The acoustical tiles were still stained darkly with God knew what. Pigeon shit, for one thing. Probably dead pigeons, as well, considering the campaign to poison them that had been initiated in the fall semester. Mal Tomlin had sworn that no one would come to Burns's rescue if the ceiling ever fell in on him.

Burns looked down at the papers again and considered picking up his pen. Then he looked at his watch.

Twenty minutes until five. Time to talk to Holt. He didn't look forward to that, but anything would be better at the moment than reading more papers.

Burns left his own office and ran the maze of other offices and small classrooms that composed the front part of the third floor. There was no one there at that hour. Clem Nelson and Miss Darling had long since gone home, and the three virtually anonymous men known to all as Larry, Darryl, and Darryl were gone as well. They came to campus, taught their classes, kept their office hours and disappeared. Some of the other faculty members complained that the three didn't carry their share of the load, but Burns liked them. At least they didn't cause him any trouble.

Holt's office was really just around the corner from Burns's own. There were two flights of stairs leading to the third floor, and Holt had his office at the head of the stairs opposite the flight Burns had come up.

The door was open; Holt was sitting at his desk, reading what looked like a comic book. There was only one window in the office, and the late afternoon sun slanted through it, giving a mellow glow to the fluorescent lighting and casting a long shadow from the potted aloe plant that sat on the wide windowsill. The wall behind Holt was covered with lobby cards from old movie serials. Holt had put the cards in acrylic frames, and Burns couldn't fault the man's taste. Burns saw Linda Stirling as *The Tiger Lady*, George Wallace as Commander Cody in *Radar Men from the Moon*, Tom Tyler in his Captain Marvel suit, and Buster Crabbe in *Space Soldiers Conquer the Universe*.

There was also a poster that said YOU CAN BE ANYTHING YOU WANT TO BE in big red letters on a white background.

Burns, who at one time or another in his life had wanted to be linebacker for the Houston Oilers, hit .400 in the major leagues, and do brain surgery, thought the poster was pretty misleading. Randy Randall, who wanted to be a lawyer, would probably have believed it, though. Burns wondered if that was good or bad.

While Burns was looking silently at the poster, Holt sensed his presence. He put down the comic book and turned to look at Burns, who glanced at the title.

"*Whiz Comics*," Holt said.

"You don't see those around much," Burns said.

"Not in English departments," Holt said. He laid a hand on the comic book. "But popular culture is quite interesting. You'd be surprised what you can learn from something like this."

"For example?" Burns said, always willing to learn something new, especially if it came from *Whiz Comics*.

Holt flipped the pages. "You can learn a lot about prejudice, for one thing." He stopped and put a finger on a picture. "Look at this."

Burns walked into the office and looked down at the comic. Holt's finger was resting just under the figure of Steamboat Willie, Billy Batson's black serving man. He had thick, heavy lips and pop eyes.

"Feets don't fail me now," Burns said.

"That's about the size of it," Holt said.

"And that's what you're teaching in your classes?" Burns asked. "Prejudice in popular culture?"

"That, among other things," Holt said. "But if you're interested, why don't you sit in someday. You could probably add a lot to the discussion."

"I might do that," Burns said.

Holt closed the copy of *Whiz Comics*. "I really wish you would," he said. "I think you and I share a lot of the same interests; I'd like to get to know you better."

Burns found himself warming to Holt, with whom he did share some interests and who certainly didn't sound like a man who had come to take over the department. He sat down in the chair by Holt's desk.

"We can start now," he said. "I've been wanting to talk to you. How have your classes been going?"

They talked about Holt's classes and Burns told him about his developmental students. They talked about movies and books and television, and Burns found himself liking Holt more and more. Eventually he edged around to the real reason for his visit.

"How is it that you wound up here?" he asked. "Not that HGC isn't a great school, but we're not exactly known for the quality of our library or our scholarship."

Holt patted the comic book. "A lot of the things I write about don't require conventional research. And for the things that do, your library is perfectly adequate. You have a very good periodicals section, and all the important books of criticism are in the stacks. You, or someone, has done a good job of keeping up."

"Thanks," Burns said. He wanted to add that Holt had not exactly answered his question, but before he could, Holt went on.

"Going to the library here isn't exactly a chore, either. Miss Tanner is most helpful, and quite attractive."

Oh no, Burns thought. *Not another rival.*

"And there's always interlibrary loan," Holt said, distracting him. "I can get books from just about anywhere. But that's not answering your question. I came here because I was asked. As simple as that."

"But surely you've been asked to go to other schools. More prestigious schools."

"True," Holt said. "But that sort of thing has never appealed to me. I'm not an academic snob."

"A lot of people are," Burns said. "And then there's the money."

"Hartley Gorman isn't exactly going to make me rich," Holt said. "But I don't need a lot of money. I have a place to live, I have access to a library, I have an office and classes to teach. What does money really matter?"

Burns didn't know what to say to that one, so he changed directions. "Dr. Partridge seems to think highly of you."

Holt nodded, frowning. "I'm sure there has been some resentment against me in the department about my teaching only three classes. I'm sorry about that. I didn't ask for the reduced load; Dr. Partridge made the offer, and I accepted. I didn't know that it would cause hard feelings."

Burns didn't say anything for a few seconds in hopes that Holt might give him some clue about why Dr. Partridge had made the offer, but it seemed that no such clue would be forthcoming.

"I don't think there's been any resentment," Burns said finally. "Well, not exactly."

"People feel that they're being treated unfairly," Holt said. "And I don't really blame them. They've been very nice about it, however."

That was the first thing Holt had said that Burns knew

wasn't true. Even Miss Darling had held herself aloof from
Holt, and Miss Darling was never intentionally aloof from
anyone. Burns had done the same thing. Under normal
circumstances, he would never have let three weeks of the
semester go by without having a conversation with a new
faculty member. He would have to have a talk with the other
instructors, ask them to try being a little friendlier.

The two men talked a while longer, and then Burns left
the office to get ready for his evening class. He was convinced
that Holt had no ulterior motives and that there was no
sinister connection between Holt and Dr. Partridge.

For a while after that day, things went more smoothly. With
a little prodding from Burns, the other members of the English department gradually got to know Holt somewhat better. They began speaking to him in the hall, having a cup of
coffee with him now and then, and discussing their classes
with him. Even Larry, Darryl, and Darryl would stop by his
office to say hello on their way in or out of the building.

All of that was fine.

What wasn't so good was the style sheet that was delivered
to everyone through the faculty mail. It contained a list of
desirable ways to refer to various groups, and it was accom-
panied by a list of "isms" that led to oppression. An
introduction at the top of the page stated that the sheet was
a product of the combined efforts of Dean Partridge and Eric
Holt. Their efforts, to put it mildly, were not appreciated by
the faculty.

"That kind of thing might go all right at some big atheistic
state university," Mal Tomlin said. "But not here at HGC."

Burns didn't think the idea should go well anywhere. He
was of the opinion that you either had freedom of speech or
you didn't. While he didn't feel it was necessary to refer to
any particular group by an unflattering or offensive name—
to use "hate speech," as it was now being called—he still
thought he should have the freedom to do so.

He thought of an old paperback that was sitting on his

shelves at home. It was by James Hadley Chase, and it was called *12 Chinks and a Woman*. Burns also had a later printing, titled *12 Chinamen and a Woman*. He supposed that if the book were to be reprinted now, it would be called *12 Asians and a Woman*. Of course, it would never be reprinted. There was no chance of that.

Another thing that disappointed Burns about the list was the noticeable (to him) absence of such terms as "redneck" and "coonass" and "white trash." Did that mean those terms were okay? In fact, there were no terms on the list that referred to white males. Maybe it was nice to know that at least one minority group was still fair game for any gibes someone might want to throw.

While the list made Burns very uncomfortable, some of Holt's ideas weren't going over well with the parents of his students, either, and Burns, as he had expected, got a number of calls. He explained that HGC was simply being innovative and trying new approaches, that a college was a forum for ideas, and that all sides were being presented so that students could judge for themselves. He hated himself for being secretly cynical about what he was saying. The list created by Dr. Partridge and Eric Holt seemed to undermine much of it, but his little speech was effective. The complaints grew less frequent.

There was no trouble about the dean's goat.

The campus seemed to be calming down and adjusting well until just after spring break, when Tom Henderson came flying out his office window, falling to his death on the sidewalk.

$\triangledown$

5

IT WAS A mild late afternoon near the end of March. There was a slight breeze that stirred the branches of the pecan trees, and already a few stars were visible in the dusky sky.

Burns had been home for a while and had just returned to the campus for his Tuesday evening class in twentieth-century American fiction. He was walking from the street toward the east entrance to Main, his mind on the list of the characteristics of post–World War II fiction that he was going to go over with his students. He hardly noticed that the pecan trees were leafing out or that the grass was so green that it would soon need mowing or that the birds were rustling around in the trees, choosing places to roost.

He was thinking about number eight on his list, "Fear of nuclear annihilation," when he heard the noise.

It was quite a noise, sticks of old, dry wood popping like pistol shots, followed by the peculiarly musical sound of shattering glass.

The windows in the offices of Main were tall, eight or ten feet high. They were divided into top and bottom halves, and either half once could have been raised or lowered. That was no longer the case; the windows had been nailed shut when the building was air-conditioned in the early 1970s. Permanently shut windows did not make for good fire safety, but they did prevent students and faculty from opening the windows and thus increasing the heating and air-conditioning bills. The long panes were all in need of new putty, and the wind rattled them in the window frames whenever it blew more than five miles an hour.

The noise Burns had heard was caused by an office window that seemed to explode outward. Shattered glass and splintered wood showered down on Burns, who, having been reared to have a healthy fear of nuclear annihilation, instinctively ducked and covered.

Above the sound of the falling glass, Burns heard Tom Henderson's scream, and before Burns even had time to look up, he heard the awful sounds of Henderson hitting the sidewalk. The one his head made was the worst.

Burns looked up then, as much to avoid looking at Henderson as to see where Henderson had come from. He thought he saw someone move in the shadows just beyond the shattered window, but he couldn't be sure.

He looked back down at Henderson. There was something runny, something reddish-gray, oozing out of the back of Henderson's head. His eyes were wide open, staring upward at the darkening sky, but Burns was sure they were not seeing it.

Burns looked away. He felt his stomach churn, and there was a warm, stinging sensation in his throat. He swallowed hard and forced himself to look at Henderson again.

Then he became aware that someone was shouting nearby and that someone else was screaming. Students on their way to evening classes were reacting to what had happened.

Only then did Burns realize that his hands hurt and that he was bleeding from cuts on his hands and arms, cuts made by the falling glass. The sidewalk where he stood was covered with glass, and there was even a glass shard lying on Henderson's stomach.

Burns swallowed again. "All of you students go inside and wait on the first floor," he said, trying to keep his voice level. He looked around for a student he knew, and his eyes lighted on a senior Bible major named Harold Kay. "Harold, I want you to dial 911. Get an ambulance. And you'd better get the police. I'll wait here until they come."

"Shouldn't you be doing something, sir?" Harold said. Students at HCG still said "sir," or some of them did. "CPR or something?"

Burns looked down into Henderson's staring eyes. "I'll try," he said, knowing it would be of no use. "You go make the call. And get everyone inside."

"Yes, sir," Harold said, as Burns knelt down beside the body and brushed the fragment of glass on Henderson's stomach to the sidewalk. It tinkled when it hit, and split into three pieces.

"Well, well, well," Chief R. M. (Boss) Napier said. "Well, well, well."

Napier was a burly man who liked leather bomber jackets and denim jeans. He had dark blond hair and a face that, with its once-broken nose and ruddy cheeks, might have been called ruggedly handsome by anyone but Burns.

There were all sorts of rumors around Pecan City about his personal life, rumors that said, for example, that he sometimes went deer hunting with only a bowie knife and a bullwhip. Burns had never been able to verify the rumors, though he wouldn't have been surprised if they were true. The things that Burns knew for a certainty, however, were much less sensational, such as the fact that Napier collected and painted miniature action figures. And that he had an eye for Elaine Tanner.

The two men were in a vacant classroom on the first floor of Main. Burns had been treated by the paramedics who came with the ambulance, and both his hands had a number of plastic bandages stuck to them. None of the cuts was deep, and none had required stitches.

Burns had sent Harold Kay up to dismiss his class, and he was sitting at a student desk, looking at Napier, who was sitting on top of the metal-and-wood teacher's desk.

"You don't really look so bad, considering," Napier said. "You're just lucky that Anderson fella didn't fall right on top of you."

"Henderson," Burns said. Napier had problems with names. "His name is Henderson."

"Was," Napier said. "His name *was* Henderson. Past tense. An English teacher should know about stuff like that. The paramedics tell me you tried to bring him back, though. You should've known it wouldn't do any good. The back of his head was cracked like a soft-boiled egg. His brains were—"

"I know," Burns said, holding up a bandaged hand to stop Napier before he went into the gory details. He'd seen Henderson's head; he didn't need to have Napier describe it. "I just thought I ought to try."

"Yeah. Well, I guess that was a good idea. No use in taking any chances."

"Did anyone tell his wife?" Burns asked.

Samantha Henderson taught typing at HGC on a part-time basis. She and her husband both taught on Tuesday evenings, but her class met in the tiny Business Building— actually nothing more than an old house converted to classroom use—which was down the street from Main.

"One of the students sent someone," Napier said. He slid to the edge of the desk and stood up. "You know, Burns, ever since I got to know you, there have been bad things happening around this college."

"Now, wait just a minute," Burns said.

Napier walked around behind Burns, who turned to look at him.

"I'm not saying it's your fault," Napier said. "It just seems to me that Pecan City used to be such a nice, quiet little place. My job used to be a whole lot easier before you started mixing in things."

"I'm sorry you're having to work so hard," Burns said.

"Sarcasm." Napier walked back to the front of the room and sat back down on the desk. "I can recognize sarcasm. My English teachers always used to be sarcastic with me."

"You can't blame me for that, either," Burns said. He found himself wondering what kind of essay Napier could write, but he pushed the thought out of his mind.

"I don't blame you," Napier said. "But I was just wondering."

"Wondering what?" Burns said.

"Well, it seems like every time something goes wrong around here, you're right in the big middle of it. First it was that business with Dean Endore—"

"Elmore," Burns said.

"Right, Elmore. And then that mess with Skeet—"

"Street," Burns said. "His name was Street."

"Sure. Street. That was it. You were right in the middle of those, weren't you."

It wasn't a question, so Burns didn't try to answer.

"Anyway," Napier went on, "what I'm betting myself is that you're up to your neck in this one, too. Am I right?"

"I don't even know what happened," Burns said. "How could I be involved in it?"

"Well, now, I don't know what happened yet, either, not for sure. The boys are still going over that office up there. But what we can speculate on is that Mr. Sanderson—"

"Henderson."

"—that Mr. Henderson either fell through that window by accident, which doesn't seem very likely; jumped through that window; or was pushed through that window."

Napier slid off the desk again and hulked over Burns. "Do you have any ideas you want to share with me about those three things, Burns? That's what you touchy-feely types like to say, isn't it? 'Share with me?' How about it, Burns?"

Burns thought about what he thought he'd seen: someone moving just out of sight beyond the broken window. But he wasn't certain he'd seen a thing. It could have been nothing at all. But he couldn't think of a reason why anyone would push Henderson through the window, much less a reason why Henderson would jump.

"I don't know any more than you do," Burns said.

"Well, that's just fine," Napier said. "That's just about what I expected you to say, Burns. And I hope it's the truth. I really do. I don't want to find myself stumbling over you while I'm investigating this case."

Burns didn't know exactly what to say to that. He could have said something like, "Who solved your last two murder cases for you?" but he didn't think that would be wise. He didn't think it would do any good to mention the shoplifting case he'd solved for Napier during the Christmas break, either, or the thefts he'd solved in the city's River Bend section during the same holiday season.

"Besides, Burns," Napier went on, "I find myself stumbling over you entirely too much these days, even when I'm not investigating a crime. Why do you think that is?"

Burns had something he could have said to that, too. He could have said, "If you'd stop following Elaine Tanner around, then you wouldn't be tripping over me all the time." But he didn't say it. Napier wasn't in a good mood, and mentioning Elaine wasn't likely to make him any happier.

"I know you've helped me out a little now and then," Napier said, relenting a little. "And I appreciate it."

He didn't sound as if he appreciated it to Burns, but Burns still said nothing. He just sat at his desk and kept his mouth shut.

"But I think it might be best if you didn't get involved in this, if you're not already. And you said you weren't involved, didn't you?"

Burns nodded. "That's what I said."

"Good. I just wanted to be sure that we understood one another. I'm going to be on the campus quite a bit investigating this death, but I don't think you and I need to run into each other at all. This Henderson wasn't in your department, and he doesn't have any connection with your department, right?"

"Right," Burns said. "Except . . ."

Napier had turned to sit on the desk again, but he whirled around. "*Except*, Burns? Except *what*?" He looked like a man who might go deer hunting with a bowie knife and a bullwhip. He looked as if he might enjoy hunting *Burns* with a bowie knife and a bullwhip.

"Nothing," Burns said.

He decided that this was not the time to mention either his own earlier suspicions of Eric Holt and Dean Partridge or Henderson's statement that he thought he recognized Holt.

Napier wasn't buying it. "Don't give me that 'nothing' crap, Burns. You had something to say. Say it."

"All right," Burns said, trying to think of a way to tell the truth while at the same time not revealing anything. "I was just about to say that in a small community like this, there are bound to be connections that aren't so obvious at first. There might be things about Henderson that we don't know."

Napier wasn't fooled by Burns's evasiveness. "What things? You'd better not be holding out on me, Burns. When I said I didn't want to be tripping over you, I didn't mean that I wanted you to hold anything back."

"I'm not holding anything back," Burns said, looking down at the top of the desk. Someone had written "Miss Darling bites the big one" there in black ink.

Napier made a sound that might have been a groan. "I just know you're going to get in my way, Burns. I just know it."

"You're still mad because I went to that basketball game, aren't you?" Burns said. "But that was two months ago. And besides, Elaine invited me."

Napier's face grew dangerously red, but then he took a deep breath and let it out slowly through his nostrils. "I'm going to forget you said that, Burns, and we're going to start all over here. I may as well face the facts. If anything happens around this campus, you're going to be in on it, no matter whether I like it or not. So tell me about this Henderson. What kind of guy was he? Who'd push him out that window?"

Burns didn't like Napier's sudden change of attitude, but he supposed that Pecan City's police force wasn't large enough for a good cop/bad cop routine. That left Napier to play both parts. Burns wondered just how much to tell him.

"You really should ask Earl Fox about him," Burns said finally. "I don't—" He stopped himself. Past tense. "I *didn't* know him very well."

"What about this new dean you've got, this Cartridge?" Napier said. "How well has she gotten to know the faculty?"

"Partridge," Burns said. "Dean Partridge. She really hasn't been here long enough to get to know everyone. I'm not sure how much help she'd be."

"I'll have to talk to her, though," Napier said. He looked at his watch—a Timex, Burns was sure. "In fact, I've got to meet her and Diller in about five minutes."

"Miller," Burns said.

"Yeah. Miller. I think he's really worried about this. He thinks there might be some bad publicity. Like I said, this used to be a nice, quiet little town. Now it's more like the murder capital of Texas."

"We don't know that he was murdered," Burns reminded him.

"No, we don't. And I hope it was all just an accident. I bet your president hopes so, too. I have to go talk to him now, but you let me know if you think of anything that could help me."

"You're sure you won't mind? I don't want you to feel that I'm interfering."

"Sarcasm again," Napier said. He walked down the aisle between the desks and out the door. Then he poked his head back in. "I'll see you around, Burns."

Burns nodded. "I'm sure you will," he said, trying a smile.

Napier looked at him for a second and then his head disappeared. He wasn't smiling.

6

IT WAS ALMOST impossible to hold classes the next day, and not just because the only thing anyone could talk about was the death of Tom Henderson. The major distraction was the "grief counseling" that Dean Partridge had ordered for any students who felt devastated by Henderson's sudden demise.

Predictably enough, very few students fell into such a group, Henderson not having been one of HGC's most popular professors. However, so that the program would not look like a terrible administrative misjudgment, all the instructors had been told to mention the special counseling sessions in their classes and encourage the students to attend them.

Burns dutifully followed orders, though he was highly suspicious of the fact that Dawn Melling had been placed in charge of the counseling. He didn't know how much good she could do.

He said as much to Fox and Tomlin as they sat in the boiler room, the only indoor "smoke-free area" left on campus where anyone felt smoking could go on undetected.

This was because the HGC's boiler was older than anyone on campus, with the possible exception of Dirty Harry, the campus security officer, who spent a great deal of his time in the boiler room, asleep.

Of course it wasn't only that the boiler was old that kept people away. It was also, like Dirty Harry, dangerous.

Dirty Harry was dangerous because he carried a big

revolver and was likely to point it at anyone who looked even the least bit out of place to him. It was a known fact that hardly anyone dared venture into a campus office on the weekend to catch up on paper grading or to map out assignments for the coming week.

Harry was likely to creep into the office behind them and throw down on them with the revolver, threatening to shoot if they didn't produce I.D. to prove they had a right to be on campus. Since HGC didn't furnish I.D. cards to its faculty, several instructors felt that they had gone through near-death experiences while looking down the barrel of Harry's .357 Magnum.

The boiler didn't carry a gun, but it was just as likely to explode as Harry's revolver, at least according to an engineering study that Dean Partridge had ordered. It was old, and if the pressure built up too much, it was going to take out half the campus. Or that was the story going around.

It was, Burns thought as he looked at it, certainly big enough. It looked a little like a stubby, asbestos-wrapped rocket ship lying there in its concrete cradles, pipes and valves extending from it and running to all the buildings it served. It was quiet for the time being, however. Thanks to the mild spring weather, the boiler wouldn't be needed to heat the campus buildings until well into the fall.

Just the same, no one came into the building that housed the boiler except for the occasional maintenance worker who was sneaking a smoke and who was therefore highly unlikely to rat on anyone else doing the same thing.

"What's Dawn going to tell the kids, anyway?" Tomlin wondered. " 'I share your pain'?"

"That's not what I'd like to share with Dawn," Earl Fox said with an attempt at a leer. His clean-cut features didn't lend themselves very well to leering, however.

"That's a sexist remark, I think," Burns told him. "I could report you to the dean for something like that."

"She might have heard that story already," Mal Tomlin said. "Not about Earl, but if what I heard is true, old

Henderson shared a thing or two with Dawn. Right, Earl?"

Fox looked the other way and tapped the ash off his cigarette onto the concrete floor. One advantage of being in the boiler room was that you didn't have to bother with an ashtray.

"Hey, Earl, is it true or not?" Tomlin asked.

To his surprise, Burns didn't know exactly what was going on. He thought he was pretty well up on the campus gossip, but this was clearly something he'd missed. And Fox clearly didn't want to talk about it.

"What's going on here?" Burns asked. "What about Henderson and Dawn?"

"I'm not supposed to say anything about it," Fox told him. "I don't know how Mal found out."

"You ought to close your office door when you've got an irate visitor," Tomlin said. "If you want to keep secrets, that is. I just happened to be passing by when Walt Melling stormed in the other day."

"I closed the door as soon as I got a chance," Fox said. "I didn't see you outside it."

"I must've been standing out of sight," Tomlin said, grinning. "I didn't hear much after you closed the door, though."

Burns was curious. "Just what did you hear?"

"I can't tell you," Tomlin said. "Didn't you hear Earl? It's a secret."

Burns looked over at Dirty Harry, who was tipped precariously back in his chair, his eyes closed, his mouth half open.

"There's no one here but us," Burns said. "And I'm not going to tell anyone."

"You'd better not," Fox said. "I haven't, not even Dean Partridge."

"I bet Walt told her, though," Tomlin said. He looked at Burns. "His face was red as a turkey's snout."

"Why?" Burns asked. "Will one of you please tell me what's going on around here?"

"You might as well tell him, Earl," Tomlin said. "He'll find out sooner or later. He's probably already helping the cops, just like he always does."

"I'm not helping the cops," Burns protested. "Boss Napier told me to keep out of it. I'm just curious."

"Sure you are," Tomlin said.

Burns could see it was useless to argue. "All right, so I'm working with the cops. Tell me what's going on, Earl, and I'll see to it that Napier doesn't take you down to the station to beat the truth out of you with his bullwhip."

"All right," Fox said. "But you didn't hear it from me." He tossed his cigarette to the floor and crushed it out.

There were a number of butts scattered around the area, and Mal Tomlin looked down at them. "If Dean Partridge ever comes in here, our ass is grass."

Fox looked even more frightened than he had at the mention of Boss Napier's legendary whip. "Can she tell they're our cigarettes?"

"Nobody but you would smoke Cost Cutters," Tomlin said.

Fox bent down and started picking up the butts. "You two help me with these. You're in this as deep as I am."

"Not until you tell me about Walt Melling," Burns said. "Then maybe I'll help you."

Fox straightened, dropping the butts back on the floor and dusting off his hands. "All right. It was last Thursday, just after Assembly. I was going through my desk to get notes for class when Melling came in. He was upset, all right. His face was just about as red as Mal said it was."

"I thought he was going to have a stroke," Tomlin said. "I mean, he was *red*."

"Why?" Burns asked, though he thought he had a pretty good idea by now.

"He said that Henderson had been hitting on Dawn," Fox said. "He said that he was going to, and I'm quoting here, 'beat the little worm to a pulp.'"

"Why come to you?" Burns asked.

"Because I'm his department chair," Fox said. "He wanted

me to have a talk with Henderson before the beating was administered. I got the idea that if I was effective, maybe the beating wouldn't even be necessary."

"Does Boss Napier know about this?" Burns asked.

"I didn't tell him," Fox said. "But I advised Henderson to go to Dean Partridge. She should know about things like that. Has Napier talked to her?"

Burns didn't know. Things wouldn't look good for Melling if Partridge remembered his feelings and reported them to Napier, however.

"What about it, Burns?" Tomlin asked. "You think it was Melling? He could've gone to Henderson's office and confronted him. Melling's a pretty big guy. He wouldn't have much trouble knocking a twerp like Henderson through a window."

"I don't know," Burns said. "Melling doesn't seem like the type."

"Anybody's the type," Tomlin said. "Besides, he probably didn't mean to kill him. He just wanted to bust him in the chops. Right, Earl?"

"Don't ask me," Fox said. He pulled out another Cost Cutter and lit it with his green Bic. "I suppose it could have happened like that."

"I bet that's just what Eric Holt wants everyone to believe," Tomlin said, getting out a Merit menthol. He lit it and blew a smoke ring.

"What do you mean by that?" Burns asked. He was beginning to wish he hadn't quit smoking.

"You're supposed to be the hotshot crime solver," Tomlin said. "You figure it out."

Burns looked out the front door of the boiler room. Students were beginning to walk by on their way to class. "We don't have all day," he said. "Why don't you just tell me."

"Maybe you've forgotten about Henderson thinking he knew Holt," Tomlin said. "But I haven't."

"I talked to Henderson about that," Burns said. "He

couldn't place Holt. Holt probably just looked like someone Henderson knew at one time."

"Or somebody he'd seen," Tomlin said. "Like on TV."

"TV?" Burns said.

" 'Unsolved Mysteries,' " Tomlin said. " 'America's Most Wanted.' "

"Oh," Burns said. Recently, Tomlin had become a devoted fan of "reality television," especially the kind of shows that related to law enforcement. He was a loyal viewer of "Cops" as well as the two shows he had just mentioned.

Then Burns thought of something else. Where had Holt been last night? He had a class in Main on Tuesday evening, but he had been nowhere to be seen during all the excitement. Burns would have to ask someone about that. He didn't think he would mention it to Fox and Tomlin, though.

Instead, he changed the subject back to Henderson. "Is there anything else you haven't told me, Earl? Anything that might be useful to the investigation, I mean?"

"What do you think might be useful?"

Burns had in mind the student he had seen running from Henderson's office earlier in the semester. "Harassment of students. That kind of thing."

"I really shouldn't talk about that," Fox said. "It's confidential."

"Not now," Tomlin said. "Henderson won't care. He's dead."

"Right," Burns said. "So what about it?"

"Well," Fox said, taking a drag off the Cost Cutter and then tossing it on the floor, "as you probably know, Henderson was a very strict grader. So naturally there have been complaints about him. There always are when someone tries to maintain high standards."

"What about other kinds of harassment?" Burns asked. "We've established that Henderson liked women."

"There's been one complaint this year," Fox said, making Burns think again of the girl who had left Henderson's office in tears. "But I'm sure that had nothing to do with Henderson's death, and I'm not going to tell you the woman's name. She wouldn't have killed anyone, and certainly not Henderson. She probably wouldn't have gone near his office with a bodyguard, much less alone."

"Did you talk to him about the woman?" Burns asked.

"Of course. He tried to pass it off as a student upset about a grade, but I think he got my message. I haven't had any complaints since then."

"Maybe no one killed him," Burns suggested. "Maybe it was an accident, or suicide."

"Sure it was," Tomlin said. "You just keep right on thinking that. But I'm betting it was murder, and I'll be surprised if that Holt wasn't mixed up in it."

Burns thought about the movement he had seen in Henderson's office. Was it just a shadow? Or had someone been in there? He wished he could be sure, one way or the other.

He was about to defend Holt again when a bell rang.

"Ten minutes till class," Tomlin said. "Gotta go."

"Me, too," Fox said. "See you later, Burns."

"Yeah," Tomlin said. "You still have a lot of stuff to tell us."

"What, for instance?" Burns asked.

"You haven't mentioned what Henderson looked like when he hit the sidewalk," Tomlin said.

"I don't think you want to know," Burns said. He didn't like to think about it, and he couldn't imagine why anyone else would want to hear such a description. But then, you never could tell about Mal.

Tomlin and Fox went out of the boiler room, but Burns stayed behind for a minute, picking up the cigarette butts, which Fox seemed to have forgotten about. Burns wasn't afraid of being caught in the company of smokers, but he didn't like to be an accomplice to litterbugs.

He tossed the butts into a trash can near the door of the boiler room and went outside, patting his palms together to get some of the ash off them. Since the night before, springtime had arrived in full force. The sun was shining, birds were singing in the pecan trees, and the air was filled with the smell of cow manure.

The maintenance crew was spreading the manure on the grounds, and Burns knew it would produce quite green grass in the near future. It always did, though the smell was certainly unpleasant for a few weeks. Franklin Miller had discovered, however, that manure was much cheaper than commercial fertilizer; in fact, it was given to the college free by Harley Gibson, a part-time teacher of agriculture courses. Harley's real job was raising cattle, and his feedlot was full of manure that he needed to get rid of. So the college got green grass, and Harley got rid of his manure. It was an arrangement that suited everyone, except maybe those who had the scent of manure in their nostrils every day.

Burns decided that on such a beautiful day there was no need to go back to his office. He didn't have a class for fifty minutes, so he had time to pay a visit to the library. What better to do on a lovely spring day?

As he walked toward the library, Burns reflected that in a way teachers lived their lives backward. For most people, spring was a beginning, and the fall was the end of something. But for teachers, spring was the end of the year.

Graduation might symbolize a new beginning for the students, but for the faculty it meant that another class was gone, with most of the students never to be seen again. Fall, with its incoming freshmen and the first days of class, was really the beginning of the adventure.

Poor Tom Henderson. Spring had really been the end of things for him. He wouldn't be seeing any more freshmen or starting any more classes. Burns supposed that he ought to pay a sympathy call on Henderson's wife, though he really didn't know her that well and he hated doing things like that. Maybe, he thought, Elaine Tanner would go with him.

7

T HE LAST PERSON Burns expected to see in the library was Boss Napier, but of course the police chief wasn't there to look at the books. He was looking at Elaine Tanner.

"I'm sorry," Burns said, stopping in the doorway of Elaine's office. "I didn't know you had company."

"That's all right," Elaine said. "R.M. and I were just talking about the case."

"Is that so?" Burns looked at Napier. The police chief was sitting in the chair by Elaine's desk, and there was a bowling trophy at his feet. He didn't appear any happier to see Burns than Burns was to see him. "What do you have to do with the case?"

Elaine pushed her glasses up on her nose. "Well, I don't really know, but I *am* associated with the college, and R.M. says that a person might know something important without realizing it."

It bothered Burns that Elaine referred to Napier as "R.M." It bothered him that she seemed to be fascinated with police work. And it bothered him that Boss Napier was sitting there in her office when it should have been obvious to anyone that she knew absolutely nothing about Tom Henderson.

He didn't say any of those things, however. He leaned casually on the door frame and said, "That's certainly interesting. Have you been able to tell the chief anything?"

"Not about the case. But we've been talking about the baseball team. Have you been to any of the games?"

Burns had not. HGC's baseball team wasn't much better

than the football team, which had won one game in the last two years. But that suddenly didn't matter to Burns.

"I've always been a baseball fan, though," he said. Napier looked at him darkly, which encouraged Burns to go on. "In fact, I played for a couple of years."

That was true. He had played second base in Little League more than twenty years before.

"Let's forget about baseball," Napier said. Burns thought the man was obviously jealous in the face of a genuine athlete. "Let's get back to the murder."

"I'd better leave," Burns said. "I don't want to get mixed up in that."

"What do you mean?" Elaine asked. "Why you're one of the best assets R.M. has here on the campus. You've helped him out more than once."

Burns smiled modestly and kept his mouth shut.

Napier wasn't smiling, but he surprised Burns by saying, "She's got a point, Burns. You remember that I told you to let me know if you found out anything? So what have you found out?"

Burns straightened a little. "You first. What makes you want to know?"

"Because it's murder now," Napier said. "We're sure of it."

Burns wasn't really surprised. That hadn't been a shadow he'd seen. Or if it had been, someone had made it.

"What makes you so certain?" he asked.

"There are a number of things that usually indicate suicide," Elaine said. "R.M. was telling me before we started talking about baseball. And this case doesn't fit the usual pattern."

I'll just bet R.M. was telling you, Burns thought. "Really?" he said. "That's very interesting. What's so different about it?"

It was Napier who answered. "In the first place, there's no note. If you kill yourself, you want everyone to know why you did it. Maybe you even want somebody to feel guilty. But we've searched Anderson's office—"

"Henderson," Burns said.

"—Henderson's office, and there's no sign of a note. That's point number one."

"What's number two?"

"Let me ask you a question," Napier said. "If you were going to kill yourself, wouldn't you open the window?"

"Those windows are pretty hard to open," Burns pointed out.

Napier agreed. "We can talk about the fire code later. But you'd find a way to open one if you wanted to jump. I've never heard of a suicide where someone jumped through a closed window."

Burns thought that was a good point. "Could it have been an accident, then?"

"I don't see how," Napier said. "Even if he fell against the window, it wouldn't break out like it did. We tested the one over his desk. You'd have to hit it pretty hard to break it."

"So what does that tell you?" Burns asked.

Elaine joined in the conversation. "Don't you see? The window ledges are low, about the level of a person's knees. Someone must have hit Tom with enough force to drive him backward and through the window."

"Is that right?" Burns asked Napier. Napier nodded. "Do you have any proof?"

Napier admitted that he didn't. "The autopsy showed that Henderson had bruises on his face that occurred before death. And not very long before. Of course his head hitting the sidewalk is what killed him. But someone probably knocked him through the window."

Burns thought about the way the back of Henderson's head had sounded when it hit. It wasn't any more pleasant to think about that now than it had been when Tomlin mentioned it earlier.

"Is there anything else?" he asked.

"Sure," Napier said. "If you were going to kill yourself, would you jump from the second floor? Why not go up to the third? Why not go up on the roof, for that matter? I know the second floor's pretty high, but if he hadn't hit the sidewalk with the back of his head like that he'd probably still be alive."

"Unless whoever hit him had already killed him," Burns said.

"Yeah," Napier agreed. "There's that."

"Who have you talked to so far?" Burns asked.

"Just Elaine—Miss Tanner," Napier said. He had the grace to look sheepish. "I just got here, so I thought I'd get her feelings on the murder."

Burns knew very well why Napier had talked to Elaine first, and it had nothing to do with getting her feelings on the murder. He thought Napier was guilty of very unprofessional behavior. Maybe there was some kind of police board that Burns could report him to.

"Who were you *planning* to talk to?" Burns asked.

"You," Napier said. "I know by now that you've nosed around and gotten mixed up in things like you always do." He tried a smile, not a pretty sight. "You can't help yourself, can you? I guess I don't blame you. It's just your character."

Without admitting anything, Burns said, "I might have heard a few things."

"I knew it. All right, Burns. Give."

"All I've heard is rumors," Burns said. He wasn't going to put Walt Melling in Napier's hands just on the basis of what had happened in Fox's office. As far as Burns knew, Melling had never gone to Henderson's office.

"I'll listen to rumors," Napier said. "Sometimes I get my best information from rumors."

"Later, maybe. What you should do is talk to Dean Partridge. She's responsible for the faculty members here."

Napier got to his feet. "Good idea. I was hoping you'd say that. For some reason she wasn't able to meet with me last night. I'm supposed to see her in her office." He looked at his watch. "In about two minutes. Want to come along?"

It was an offer Burns couldn't refuse.

* * *

Dean Partridge's office was on the second floor of the library. The outer office was manned—or personed, Burns thought, trying to be politically correct—by Norma Tunnage, the dean's secretary.

"Hello, Dr. Burns," Norma said. "Did you want to see the dean?"

Burns said that he did, and Norma announced him on the intercom. She made no mention of Napier, who wasn't, after all, college personnel.

Burns opened the door to the inner office. Dean Partridge's desk was directly opposite the door, and there was a tall bookshelf behind it filled with old textbooks and spiral-bound notebooks. The desk was oak, and the dean's chair was red leather. The room's other furniture consisted of a leather couch, a low coffee table, and a leather chair.

Dean Partridge looked much as always, or maybe a little more severe than usual because her long hair was pulled straight back and coiled into a bun on the back of her head. She got up from behind her desk when they walked into the room.

"Good morning, Dr. Burns," she said. "What can I do for you this morning?"

"It's not me you can do something for," Burns said. "This is Bo—Chief Napier of the Pecan City police. He's here to talk to you about Tom Henderson."

Partridge walked around her desk and shook hands briskly with Napier. "Of course. Poor Tom. His death was quite a shock to all of us. He was an asset to the college. Why don't you two have a seat, so we can talk? I'll have Norma bring in some coffee."

Burns didn't like coffee after seven in the morning, but he didn't protest. If the dean wanted coffee, he'd drink it. He and Napier sat on the couch, and Partridge sat behind her desk to call Norma.

The coffee arrived, and Norma served everyone. Burns wondered if it would have been politically correct for a male dean to ask Norma for coffee. Maybe it didn't matter.

Burns sipped his coffee slowly and carefully. It was too hot to drink. After a few seconds of awkward silence, Napier broached the subject of Tom Henderson's death, going through much the same explanation that he had just gone over with Burns and Elaine.

Dean Partridge set her coffee cup down on the saucer with a clink. "Murder," she said after a few seconds. "Do you have any suspects, Chief Napier?"

Napier shook his head. "Not a one. We're just beginning our investigation. I hope we'll have your full cooperation."

"Of course you will. Just exactly how do you think I can help?"

"Well, you can start by telling me if you know of anyone on the faculty who might've wanted Henderson out of the way."

"Oh, no. Of course not. I've been here only a few months, but I can say that the mutual respect the members of this faculty have for one another is unparalleled in my experience."

Napier looked puzzled.

"That means no one here has any enemies," Burns said.

Napier wasn't impressed. "I know what she means, Burns. But I also know what goes on around this place, what with that dean getting knocked off not so long ago, and then that writer who used to teach here. I just don't believe all that 'respect' stuff."

Dean Partridge sat up rigidly. "Are you implying that I might not be telling the truth about this faculty?"

Napier shrugged. "It's your faculty. You can think what you want to. I'm just talking about past history. And like you say, you haven't been here that long."

"Dr. Henderson's death has nothing to do with the past," Dean Partridge said—a little too quickly, Burns thought.

"How do you know?" Napier asked.

Partridge seemed slightly flustered, which surprised Burns. He wouldn't have thought anything could bother her. "Well," she said, "it just couldn't."

Napier didn't press her. "You never know about murder.

But what you're telling me is that you never had any problems with Henderson, and you don't know of anyone who did. Is that about right?"

Dean Partridge pushed at her bun with her right hand. "That is correct."

Burns wondered if the dean was telling the truth and decided that she was. Earl Fox must not have convinced Walt Melling to see the dean about his complaint. Whether Melling had gone on to see Henderson was another question.

"That's what Miller told me about Henderson last night," Napier said. "He was a wonderful professor, Miller said. Loved by one and all."

That sounded like Miller, all right, Burns thought, and Melling certainly wouldn't have gone to the president about his troubles. Miller didn't like people who did anything to upset the smooth operation of the college, and everyone knew it.

Napier talked to the dean for several more minutes, but Burns found his attention wandering. It was clear that the police chief wasn't going to get anything out of her. Either she didn't know anything or she was adept at lying.

After they had left the office and were walking down the stairs to the first floor, Napier said, "She knows something."

Burns stopped on the landing. "How can you tell?"

"You saw the way she looked when I said something about what's happened here in the past. There might be a connection."

"But *she* wasn't here in the past," Burns said.

"I know that. But it bothered her anyway. That's something you can check into."

"Me?" Burns was incredulous. *"Me?"*

Napier looked around the dimly lit landing. "I don't see anybody else standing here. Do you?"

"But you told me to stay out of things. You said—"

Napier put up a hand. "I know what I said, and so do you. I was a little upset at first, but after that I said you were going to get mixed up in this no matter whether I wanted you to or not. I said it was in your nature, that you just couldn't help it. Don't tell me you can't remember that."

"All right," Burns said. "I remember."

"And I practically told Elaine that you'd been a big help in the past. You remember that, too, don't you?"

Burns didn't remember that the conversation had gone exactly that way, but he said. "I remember."

"I thought so. What do you want me to do next? Beg you to help? Because I'm not going to do that. If you want to help, fine. If you don't, then just keep out of the way."

"I'll help if I can," Burns said.

"Good," Napier said.

They started on down the stairs. When they reached the lobby of the library, Napier said, "You don't need to question Elaine, though. I'll handle that part of it."

Burns thought Napier might be making a joke, and though he wasn't sure, he smiled anyway. "We'll see about that. What did you have in mind for me, then?"

"First, find out about your dean's past connections with people on this campus. After you do that, we've got a list of names you can look at, everyone who was in the building last night. I'll have my men check it out, but it won't do us any good."

"Why not?"

"Because you know as well as I do that whoever killed Henderson got out of there before their name was on any list."

Burns wondered again where Holt had been. "So you want me to find out who else was in the building?"

"That's right. And keep your ears open for any gossip about somebody who might've had it in for Henderson."

Burns wondered if this was the time to say something about Walt Melling, but he decided against it. He'd talk to Walt first and see if there was anything in the story. Maybe Earl had gotten him calmed down and he had never confronted Henderson at all.

"Anything else?" Burns asked.

"That ought to do it for now. Are you going back to your office?"

Burns had planned to go back to the library for a private visit with Elaine. "Maybe. Why?"

"I thought I'd walk part of the way with you," Napier said. "Just to make sure you get there."

Oh well, Burns thought. *If I don't get to see Elaine, he won't either.*

They left the building together.

8

NAPIER DIDN'T GO all the way to Main with Burns. His car was parked on the street on the east side of the building, and he turned away down the sidewalk. Burns watched him get in the car and drive away, then almost went back to the library. But he thought he might as well go into the counselors' area and see how the grief counseling was going. And to talk to Dawn Melling if he got the chance.

He went into Main and narrowly avoided running into Rose, who was sweeping the hallway just inside the door.

"Look out, Doctah Burns," Rose said. "You gonna run somebody down if you don't be more careful."

"Sorry, Rose," Burns said. "I was thinking about something."

Rose nodded vigorously, causing her wig to slip a little to one side. It was a terrible wig, and Burns had never seen her without it. He had no idea why she wore it, however, and he wasn't going to ask.

"You thinkin' 'bout that murder last night, like all the rest of us. This place gettin' dangerous, Doctah Burns. Real dangerous."

"Murder?" Burns said. "What makes you think it was murder?"

"Evahbody know it's a murder," Rose said. She started sweeping down the hall, shaking her head as she went. "This a bad place. A bad place."

She had a point there, Burns thought. He wondered what the average mortality rate at small colleges was and decided that HGC was certainly doing nothing to lower it.

He walked on down to the counseling office and went inside. This time, Dawn Melling was not there to meet him. Instead there was a student secretary, a young woman who had been in one of Burns's classes.

"Hello, Stephanie," Burns said. "Is Ms. Melling in?"

Stephanie was a tall, thin blond with an overbite. "She's doing grief counseling today, Dr. Burns."

Burns knew that. "I was wondering if I could see her. If she's not too busy, that is."

Stephanie looked serious. "She's not too busy. I don't think there's anyone with her at all. She's in her office, if you want to talk to her."

The counselors' offices were down a narrow carpeted hallway from the main office. Burns walked down the hall and tapped on Dawn's door.

A muffled voice said, "Come in."

Burns opened the door. Dawn was sitting at her desk, reading a paperback book: *When Bad Things Happen to Good People*. She put the book down. "Hello, Dr. Burns. Would you like to talk about Dr. Henderson's death?"

That wasn't why Burns had come in, but it was as good an excuse as any for staying a few minutes. "Yes, if you don't mind."

"That's what I'm here for. Please have a seat."

Burns sat in the chair by Dawn's desk and looked at her. She was wearing what Burns supposed was her mourning outfit: a tight black dress; black shoes with heels that seemed to Burns inappropriately high; and what looked like a tiny piece of black lace attached to her hair. Her fingernails and lips were as red as ever, and she looked even more like Elvira than usual.

"You know, Dr. Burns," she said, achieving eye contact, "death is a frightening thing to some people, but we all have to get our fears out in the open and talk about them. That's the first step."

First step to what? Burns wondered. "I'm sure that's true. But I'm not really experiencing any fear."

"Anxiety, then? When men get to be a certain age, they realize that they don't have many more years of life left and that they probably haven't achieved the dreams they had when they were young. That can be very depressing to some people."

It certainly could, Burns thought, though he hadn't considered himself as being at that age. Dawn really knew how to cheer a fellow up. She was a regular little Miss Pollyanna Sunshine. No wonder she'd been asked to do the grief counseling.

"I'm not depressed, Dawn," he said. "How about Walt?"

"Walt? What does Walt have to do with anything?"

"That's what I was wondering. I mean, a man who hasn't achieved his dreams might get frustrated and take out his frustrations on others. Do you think Walt might ever do anything like that?"

Dawn wasn't looking at Burns now. She toyed with the book on her desk, squaring it with the border of her desk calendar. Burns was impressed with her desk. There was no clutter. Just the calendar, a pen, and a pad for writing. And the book.

"Walt is a very secure person," Dawn said.

"I'm sure he is. But I've heard some disturbing things lately. . . ." Burns let his voice trail off.

"They're not true," Dawn said, her voice rising. "Whatever you've heard, it's just gossip."

"Then there's no need for you to get upset. And I'm sure none of it was your fault. You're a very attractive woman, and I'm not surprised that Tom Henderson made a pass at you."

"Oh!" Dawn's mouth was a soft red circle. "Who told you that? Did you tell Walt? I know you're a friend of that policeman, that Boss Napier. Did you tell him about Walt? Did you?"

"No," Burns said, almost overwhelmed by the rush of words. "I haven't told anyone, but I think you should let me know what happened. If Boss Napier does hear about Walt, maybe I can do something to help."

Dawn reached out and grabbed Burns's hand. "Oh, thank you, Dr. Burns. You don't know how much something like that means to a person. An offer to help, I mean. So many people these days just don't care any more than a gun about others."

Any more than a *what?* But Burns didn't allow himself to be distracted. "So Walt isn't quite as secure as you said?"

"No. He's not. And I don't know why. He knows that I would never, ever look at another man."

As she spoke, Dawn looked straight into Burns's eyes. She hadn't let go of his hand, either.

"I'm sure you wouldn't," Burns said, retrieving his hand. "But Walt might not know that."

"I've told him and told him. But he was a football player, you know. He has this idea that he has to prove himself."

Small-college All-American, as Burns recalled. Back in the glory days of HGC football. And that was the main reason Melling had been hired as the college's head of recruiting. He could speak with authority about the time when a tiny school in the heart of Texas had teed it up with the big boys and come out on top, if not every time, at least some of the time.

"He thought he had to prove himself to Tom Henderson?"

"I know, I know. It sounds ridiculous. Tom is so small, and Walt is so big. Walt should have known how foolish it was to let a little remark get him so upset. But he was determined to do something."

"What remark?" Burns asked.

"Oh, dear. Do I really have to tell you?"

She didn't, of course, but Burns's curiosity was aroused. "It might help," he said.

Dawn didn't need any further encouragement. "I was in the outer office alone one afternoon when Tom—Mr. Henderson—came by. He said something about my . . . figure."

"What did he say?"

"He said . . . he said, 'That's quite a set you've got there, Dawn.' "

Now there was political incorrectness for you, Burns thought. Or maybe it was just stupidity, since Henderson certainly should have known better. It wasn't as if every faculty member didn't get memos each semester about sexual harassment and exactly what constituted it. They did. And recent memos from Dean Partridge had expanded on that theme at length.

But Tom Henderson had been a throwback to a time when men thought women liked to hear that kind of thing, though Burns was no longer sure there had ever been such a time. He was beginning to believe that though women might have tolerated such remarks in the past, they had probably always held men like Henderson in contempt for making them.

On the other hand Henderson, like Walt Melling, might have thought he had something to prove—to himself, to women, to the world in general. It was hard to judge people without knowing them better, and no one was ever going to get to know Tom Henderson any better, not now.

Burns got his mind back on track. "And Walt threatened to do something to Tom? Like beat him up?"

"Yes, but he didn't really mean it. He gets mad like that sometimes, but in a few days he gets over it. You know how that is."

Burns didn't really know, but he nodded anyway. "And did he get over it this time?"

"I guess," Dawn said, but Burns could tell that she wasn't sure. "He told me that he was going to confront Tom, but he never said whether he did or not. So I guess he didn't."

Or maybe he didn't want to talk about knocking Henderson through his office window during the confrontation, Burns thought. He said, "Where was Walt last night?"

Dawn didn't even have to think about it. "Oh, he was at home with me. We watched TV. 'Coach' and 'Roseanne.' Those are our favorite shows."

Burns wasn't a TV watcher. "What time did he get home?"

There was a clock on the office wall. Dawn looked at it as if it might tell her something. "About six thirty. He had to stay late and work on some expense sheets."

Six thirty. Henderson had landed on the walk at about six fifteen. And Melling lived only a short distance from the campus, which meant that he could have clobbered Henderson, left Main, and gotten home by six thirty with no trouble at all.

"Was he upset when he got home?" Burns asked.

Dawn looked surprised at the question. "Well, of course he was. Wouldn't you be if someone got killed right outside where you were working?"

"I'm sure I would. But was Walt questioned by the police?"

"No. He said there was nothing he could tell them. And he was too upset by what had happened to stay here at school. So he just came home."

Burns considered that. It was possible. It was even more than likely, if Melling had thought he might somehow be implicated because of his earlier statements about Henderson. He wouldn't have wanted to stay around Main and talk to the police even if he were innocent.

"Did he want to talk about it?" Burns asked. "Tom's death, I mean."

"Yes. He knows I'm very good at helping with things like that. I have a way with soothing the savage breasts."

Burns started to say something, but thought better of it. Dawn was simply guilty of a slight misquotation, and not an uncommon one, though Burns had never heard the matter put precisely that way.

He said, "I'm sure you do. And did Walt seem all right after you talked things over?"

"He certainly did. He slept like a bug."

Burns caught himself before he asked exactly what *that* meant. "And he came to work today?"

"Yes. He has a recruiting trip tomorrow, and he had to get things set up."

"I should probably talk to him," Burns said. "It might get his mind off his troubles."

"Oh, would you?" Dawn took Burns's hand again and gave him a confidential look. "It might be good for him to talk to another man. Sometimes there are things you might not want to discuss with your wife."

Burns got his hand back. "I'll talk to him. I know that your talking to me has helped me deal with things."

"I'm glad," Dawn said. "To tell the truth, you're the first person who's come in for grief counseling all day."

"If I see Dean Partridge, I'll tell her how much it meant to me."

"Thank you. And please do go by and see Walt."

"Don't worry," Burns told her. "I will."

Walt Melling's office was quite close to Dawn's—practically on the other side of the wall, in fact—but to get there Burns had to leave the counseling area and go back out into the main hallway. Then he had to go through another glass door to the recruiting office.

The sad truth was that Hartley Gorman College, unlike the big state-supported universities, the schools of the Ivy League, certain other prestigious colleges, and the well-known party schools, didn't get its pick of the nation's high-school graduates. In fact, HGC had to scratch for nearly every entering freshman it got.

Not that things were as bad as they had been under the previous administration. Franklin Miller was a master of public relations as well as a shrewd money-raiser, and he had improved both the school's image and its financial situation. However, that didn't mean it was easy to persuade students to attend a small liberal arts college with no national reputation, a losing football team, and a location that might best be described as out-of-the-way.

All of which meant that it was necessary to have a staff of full-time recruiters, men and women who traveled around the state to attend College Nights at high schools from the Red River to the Rio Grande, setting up at a card table and passing out college catalogs and pamphlets praising the virtues of the small liberal arts college.

And since HGC was a denominational school, it helped if the recruiters had certain talents beyond the ability to glad-hand high school seniors and their parents. Being able to sing a solo at the local church's Sunday service was a real plus. A talent for preaching didn't hurt, either.

Or, like Walt Melling, you could be a former football hero with a full head of wavy black hair, soulful brown eyes, and only the tiniest beginning of a paunch to signal that the stomach muscles were finally loosening up a tad.

Coach Thomas, Melling's best friend, was in the recruiting office when Burns entered. Thomas and Melling were swapping football stories. Thomas had once tried out for offensive center with the Houston Oilers, and while he hadn't survived training camp, he was as close to a pro as anyone in Pecan City knew. Melling had been neither drafted nor signed as a free agent. He was good enough for small college ball, but he was too slow for the big boys.

The walls of the office were decorated with black-and-white photos of Walt in his college football glory. There was an obviously posed shot of Walt leaping gazellelike through the air, offering a perfect stiff-arm to a nonexistent tackler. Another showed him receiving a flawless pass from an invisible quarterback. Yet another was a head-on shot of Walt charging down the field, eyes narrowed, nostrils flared, teeth clenched.

Burns thought all three were excellent photos, but he thought they would have been considerably more realistic if only Walt had been wearing a helmet in them.

"Hey, Burns," Thomas said. "Conjugated any tough verbs lately?"

Thomas was always saying something like that, but Burns didn't hold it against him. He didn't really mean anything by it. Actually, he was quite fond of Burns, who had gotten him out of a jam after the murder of Dean Elmore the previous year.

"How does the recruiting for next year's team look, Coach?" Burns asked.

"Going great. I was just telling Walt that if we can sign that kid from Pecos, Ralph Rippon, we'll be in the tall cotton. None of the big schools want him because he's only five foot four, but he's faster than a mule deer. He'll be an all-conference receiver his freshman year, you hide and watch."

"Do you believe that, Walt?" Burns asked.

"Huh? What?" Melling obviously hadn't been paying the least attention. His mind was on something else, maybe on his recruiting trip, but somehow Burns didn't think that was the case.

"That Ralph Rippon will be all-conference his freshman year."

"Oh, yeah, quite a kid. An honor student, too. You'll get him, Coach. Don't sweat it."

Thomas left the office with a smile, obviously lost in dreams of a winning team. Burns thought it would be nice if the Panthers could just break even one year.

"It's not like it was when you were playing," Burns told Melling.

Melling nodded. "Nope. But that was before everybody wanted to go to school where there were shopping malls and movie theaters on every corner."

"Is that what they're looking for?"

"I guess so. I don't really know, to tell you the truth. But the old idea of a little school where everybody's somebody doesn't sell like it used to."

Looking for a way to change the subject, Burns glanced out the office window. He could see the sidewalk where Henderson had landed.

"Nice view," he said.

Melling was looking too. "Sometimes."

"Not last evening, though."

"No."

This wasn't getting them anywhere. Burns decided to take a more direct approach. "I heard that you and Tom had a little disagreement not long ago."

Melling hadn't asked Burns to sit down. They both stood there looking out the window. There were two students coming up the walk, a man and a woman. They both stopped and looked down at the approximate spot where Henderson had hit the concrete. Rose or someone had hosed down the walk to clean off the bloodstains, but Burns suspected that there might still be signs of Henderson's sudden demise. After a second or two the man pointed to the second-floor window. The two students looked up for a while, then shook their heads and walked on into the building.

"I wasn't the only one who had a disagreement with Tom," Melling said. "Lots of people didn't like him."

"Who?" Burns asked.

"You should know. One of your faculty members told him that he'd better stop asking questions about him."

Burns didn't have to ask who Melling meant. "Did you see Tom fall?"

"No. I was working at my desk. I didn't know a thing about it until I heard all the commotion."

"And then you just went home."

Melling turned his head slightly and looked at Burns. "That's right. I saw that you were there, and I didn't think there was anything I could do to help."

Burns knew that he could have been seen from either the window they were standing in front of or the one in Henderson's office, but he didn't think Melling was going to say which one he'd seen Burns from.

"About your disagreement with Tom," Burns said.

"That's all it was. Just a disagreement. I didn't kill him, if that's what you're getting at. I know you're in tight with the police."

That *had* been what Burns was getting at, more or less, but he didn't want to admit that to Melling. He didn't want to admit to being "in tight with the police," either.

"I didn't mean to be prying," he said. "I was just curious about your reaction to Tom's death, considering what he said to your wife."

Melling turned his entire body toward Burns. His face didn't look nearly so handsome now. "You know what he said?"

"Well, not really. Just sort of generally. I mean, I didn't hear him say it. So how could I know what he said?"

Melling's face didn't change. The hands that had carried a football for more than a thousand yards two seasons in a row were balled into fists. "Nobody says things like that about my wife. Not if I find out about it."

"I don't blame you for being angry," Burns told him. "Not that I know what Tom said, mind you, but I'm sure it wasn't pleasant."

"People shouldn't say things like that. Especially not if they teach at a religious school."

"You're right," Burns said. "You're absolutely right. Well, I know you have to get ready for that big recruiting trip, and I have a class. I'll see you around, Walt."

Walt didn't say anything to that, and Burns left before he thought of something. Walt really didn't look much like his old photos anymore, except for the one where he was charging down the field.

Burns wondered if a man like that would be capable of throwing Tom Henderson from a window and decided that he probably would.

9

SAFELY IN HIS office, Burns opened the center drawer of his desk and pulled out a piece of paper and an old Parker T-Ball Jotter that he liked. He started making a little list, trying to get his thoughts organized. The list was headed by Tom Henderson's name, and beneath the name Burns wrote what he knew.

> 1. Eric Holt wasn't around the building the night Tom Henderson died. Or if he was, no one seems to have seen him.
> 2. Melling says that Holt threatened Tom because Tom was asking questions about Holt. (Melling didn't use Holt's name, but that's who he meant.)

Burns stopped writing and looked out his office window. There was a lizard sunning itself on the cracked stone windowsill outside. Burns wasn't particularly interested in the lizard. He was interested in what questions Henderson had been asking about Holt. And whom he had been asking. Burns would see if he could find out. He looked down at his list and began writing again.

> 3. Walt Melling was clearly infuriated with Tom for making remarks to Dawn. He's still upset about it.
> 4. There had been a complaint against Henderson made by a female student.

Burns stopped writing again and clicked the Jotter a couple of times. He was going to have to talk to Earl Fox about that student. Fox hadn't revealed the student's name, which was the proper and professional thing, of course, but the fact that Henderson had definitely been murdered changed the picture. As far as questioning the student went, Burns rightly or wrongly considered himself a little more sensitive than Boss Napier. Better for Burns to talk to her than for Napier to find out about her first. Burns would talk to Fox later and get the name.

5. Henderson thought he might know Holt, but couldn't remember where he might have met or seen him.

That one went along with number 2, and Burns drew an arrow connecting the two entries.

6. People suspect that there might be some tie between Dean Partridge and Holt. Why else would Holt have come to HGC?

Burns stared down at the list. Was that all? It didn't seem like much to go on, but he would do what he could with it. There was something else that was bothering him, something that someone had said or done, but he couldn't pull it out of his memory. Maybe it would come to him later.

He put the list in his desk drawer along with the pen and started grading some papers from his developmental students. He used a green pen for that.

Some of the students had actually improved over the course of the semester. Burns wasn't sure whether the improvement was due to his teaching skills or whether the students had finally managed to absorb something through some mysterious process of osmosis. After all, it seemed nearly impossible that they could have sat in classrooms for nearly thirteen years now without learning anything about how a sentence was put together.

After a few minutes of grading, he decided to discard the osmosis theory. If anything good had happened, he was going to take credit for it himself.

By early that afternoon, Burns was feeling good. He had put Henderson's murder out of his mind and had graded all his papers; some of the students had even made A's. Burns leaned back in his desk chair and told himself that he was a pretty fair teacher even if he did say so himself, which he had to do, since no one else at HGC was going to say it for him. So far, Dean Partridge hadn't been one to lavish praise on the faculty.

And while he hadn't solved Henderson's murder, he was making progress, wasn't he? He had made a list, and he was convinced that getting his thoughts down was an orderly first step, necessary in the investigative process.

He looked out the window. The sun had moved, and so had the lizard, probably having slithered down a convenient crack in the wall. Burns thought it was just about time to go home.

But then George (The Ghost) Kaspar came moping through Burns's office door.

"What's the trouble, George?" Burns asked, struck by the young man's gloom. George had never been the despondent type before, not even in the depths of a losing football season.

"It's Bunni," George said. "And it's all your fault, Dr. Burns."

That didn't sound promising. Burns wondered where the lizard had gone and whether it needed any company in its crack in the wall. Probably not.

"Sit down, George," he said trying to sound cheerful for George's benefit. "Tell me what I've done."

George sat heavily. "You made us read that poem last year," he said.

That cleared things up, all right.

"What poem?" Burns asked. He had assigned quite a few poems in the class George had taken. Dozens probably.

George was looking at the floor, his hands clasped between

his knees. He was the very picture of dejection. "The one about the woman."

Burns wasn't catching on. There were lots of poems about women. "What woman, George? Remember what I said in class about being specific?"

George did not admit remembering. "You know which woman. The one who walked in beauty. Like the night."

"Oh," Burns said. "That poem."

George looked up. "I really liked that poem, Dr. Burns. Maybe you couldn't tell in class, but I really did."

"It's a very fine poem," Burns said. He didn't know what else to say.

"It reminded me of Bunni."

Burns just sat there. He couldn't tell where this was leading, and he couldn't think of a response.

"Did you ever memorize a poem?" George asked.

Burns had memorized many poems in his youth, some of them because he was required to and others because he liked them. Not many people did that these days.

"Yes," he said. "I've memorized a poem or two."

"Well, I hadn't. Never, not even in grade school. But I memorized that one."

"I'm glad to hear it. You should be proud of yourself, not depressed."

"I'm not depressed because I memorized the poem. I'm depressed because it got me in trouble with Bunni."

"How?" Burns asked. He really didn't see how memorizing a poem could get anyone into trouble.

"She says I'm oppressing her."

Uh-oh, Burns thought. "Didn't we decide earlier in the semester that you weren't oppressing her? You were oppressing other people, but not her."

"Yeah, but that was then. Now *she's* feeling oppressed. And all because of that poem."

"I don't think I see the connection," Burns said.

"Well, the reason I memorized that poem was because it reminded me of Bunni, so I said it for her. 'She walks in

beauty, like the night | Of cloudless climes and starry skies.'
Bunni's like that, Dr. Burns."

Bunni was a little too young for Burns's tastes, but he
could see how a young man like George might be affected
that way, though he was a little surprised at George's
sensitivity. He hadn't thought the boy had it in him.

Burns himself, when he was very much younger, had once
recited a few lines of the same poem to a young woman of
his acquaintance, and the effect had been quite satisfactory.
But that had been in another country; he didn't know what
had happened to the wench (and what a politically incorrect
term *that* was), but he certainly hoped she wasn't dead.

"Bunni didn't appreciate your recitation?" he said.

"She sure didn't. She said all I thought about was the way
she looked and that I didn't care anything about her 'inner
beauty.' "

This didn't look good. Burns asked if George had affirmed
Bunni's inner beauty.

George gave a glum nod. "I told her I thought she was
sweet."

Burns felt a little sorry for George, who was probably a lot
more at home on the football field than in trying to deal with
a young woman who has suddenly discovered sexism.

" 'Sweet' probably wasn't the right word to pick," he said.

"No," George said. "It sure wasn't. It just made her
madder."

He sighed and stared at the worn carpet. Burns couldn't
think of anything comforting to say, so he didn't say
anything at all. After a minute or so of gloomy silence,
George looked up.

"She's going to bring charges against me," he said.

"Charges?" Burns found that hard to believe. "Did you do
something stupid, George? Besides reciting the poem, I
mean."

But George hadn't done anything stupid. "Not charges
like the police arrest you for. She's taking me to the student
court for 'looksism,' whatever *that* is."

Burns groaned inwardly. "Looksism" had been the subject of one of Dean Partridge's memos, in which she had discussed the evils of basing an opinion of a person on that person's appearance. Most frequently, looksism took the form of liking a person for his or her personal beauty.

"But I don't see anything wrong with that," George said after Burns had explained it to him. "How else are you going to get an opinion of someone you don't know? You kind of like their looks, don't you? That's what makes you want to get to know them better."

"I suppose it works that way sometimes," Burns said, thinking of Elaine Tanner. He had wanted to get to know her better as soon as he saw her. Boss Napier had wanted to get to know her better, too, but Burns wasn't going to dwell on that topic.

"Then later on you find out stuff about them," George said. "Maybe you find out they're selfish or something like that and you don't ask them out again. But that's not the way it worked with Bunni."

"You found out she was sweet."

"Sure. But that just made me like her even more. I don't get it, Dr. Burns. What's wrong with being pretty and sweet?"

"Nothing," Burns said, but he wasn't sure that he was right.

The world he was living in wasn't at all like the world he had grown up in and grown more or less familiar with. Women these days didn't seem to want to be pretty and sweet. They wanted to be autonomous and tough. Or maybe not. Burns was clearly out of his depth. He felt the way a semi-intelligent dinosaur might have felt while studying the first mammals.

"Are you sure Bunni's going to bring this up before the student court?" he asked.

"Yes. Just like I was caught cheating on a test or something. I've never cheated at anything in my life, Dr. Burns."

"I'm sure you haven't. Maybe we could get someone to

talk to Bunni about this. I think you're willing to try to
understand her point of view, aren't you?"

"I guess so," George said. "If I can."

"Good. Then she should certainly be willing to do the
same for you."

Burns tried to think of someone Bunni might talk to. Miss
Darling was still in her office, but Burns was pretty sure that
Miss Darling wouldn't have any more of a clue to what was
going on than he did. Clem might, but she had already gone
home.

Dawn Melling was still in the counseling office, however.
Burns didn't have much confidence in her advice, but she
was a certified counselor.

"We'll ask Bunni to talk to Ms. Melling," he said. "Do
you know where she is right now?"

"I think it's too late for that," George said. "She's already
talking to somebody."

Uh-oh. "Who?" Burns asked.

"Miss Tanner."

Burns groaned again. This time he did it aloud.

"Bunni's right, you know," Elaine Tanner said. She was
sitting at her desk, surrounded by her trophies.

"Maybe," Burns said. If he got into an argument with
Elaine, he didn't want it to be about Bunni and George.

"There's not really any 'maybe' about it. Do you see all
these trophies?"

Burns thought about saying that, no, he didn't see any
trophies. Were there supposed to be trophies around? But
Boss Napier had already caught him using sarcasm.

"I see them."

"And I told you why I have them, didn't I?"

"To increase your self-esteem, you said."

"That's right. And why do you think I might need to do
that?"

Since Burns had only recently been wondering the same
thing, he said, "I have no idea."

"You wouldn't." Elaine looked at him with something like pity. "That's because you're a man."

"I don't see why being a man has anything to do with it."

"Naturally. That's because you've never had to prove that you're something more than a pretty face. You've never sat in a class without being called on because you were a cute redhead whom the professor thought was dumb as a post without ever having spoken a word to you."

Burns would have liked to dwell on the fact that Elaine had more or less admitted that she was a cute redhead, but he didn't think that would be smart.

"I try to call on everyone in my classes," he said. "I probably go out of my way to call on the women."

"I believe you."

There was some comfort in that, at least, but there was no consolation in what Elaine had to say next.

"I suppose you realize that calling on the women as often as the men makes you an exception. Studies have shown that even female teachers don't call on women nearly as often as they call on the males in the class."

"I've read about that. But how does it explain the trophies?"

"No one ever called on me, even when I knew the answers. And I *always* knew the answers, which is more than I can say for most of the people, the *male* people, who did get called on. And that didn't do a lot for my self-esteem. By the end of my undergraduate academic career, I needed more than just a bunch of guys calling me for dates to boost my ego."

"There were a bunch of guys calling you for dates?"

Elaine waved a hand, dismissing all the calls. "Yes. But that doesn't have anything to do with it. Later on, when I went to library school, the majority of students were women. I got called on a lot more often. But it was too late; the damage was already done."

Burns was beginning to catch on. "You started buying the trophies about then, I suppose."

"That's right. I needed something to affirm my self-worth,

and I thought having the tangible signs of success around might help, even if I hadn't really earned them myself."

"The Cowardly Lion," Burns said.

Elaine smiled. "Leave it to an English teacher to relate everything to literature."

"Not everyone would consider *The Wizard of Oz* to be literature," Burns said. He was thinking that Eric Holt would, maybe, except that Frank L. Baum had the misfortune to have been a white male.

"That's their misfortune, then. I think it's a wonderful story. But we're getting off the subject, aren't we?"

Burns supposed that they were, but they hadn't drifted too far. "So you think Bunni, having been judged on her appearance, is going to suffer the way you did?"

"I would say that it's possible."

"But this is different. It doesn't have anything to do with her classes, and George said that her appearance was important to him only at first. After he got to know Bunni, he began to appreciate her better qualities."

"She told me. He thinks she's *sweet*."

"Is there something wrong with that?" Burns knew what he thought. He wanted to hear Elaine's views on the subject.

"Maybe not, if there's more to it. But if that's all George sees, he's guilty."

"Guilty of looksism?"

"Of more than that, whatever it is. He's guilty of looking for June Cleaver or Harriet Nelson instead of a real person."

"And I don't suppose women are looking for Ward or Ozzie, either."

"Not most women."

Burns thought that was too bad. Ozzie and Ward seemed to him to represent ideal husbands. He'd always hoped that if he ever got married and had a family, he could be like either man, both of whom always seemed to be available and able to solve any family crisis with a short man-to-man talk with the kids, none of whom, come to think of it, had been

daughters. Now it seemed that Burns had adopted the wrong
role models.

But then he'd always suspected that. The unmarried
women in movies and on TV never went for the clean-cut
guys who followed the rules. They always went for James
Dean or his latest wannabe. Luke Perry, lately.

It was the same in fiction. Sid Sawyer could never be the
hero of a novel, though Tom could. And Huck Finn was even
better.

"You don't think Bunni will change her mind?" Burns
asked.

"Are you asking me to help her change it?"

While Burns might have had that in the back of his mind
earlier, he knew better than to admit it. "I just thought
someone might help her to see George's point of view."

"I don't think I can do that. I'm afraid I believe George's
point of view is based pretty much on what Bunni says it is."

"Would it help if you talked to George?"

"I don't think so. You've explained his views very well."

Burns didn't remember having explained George's views
at all, but he could hear a bugle in the back of his head
blowing retreat. So he got out of there.

10

THE NEXT DAY was HGC's annual Spring Frolic. There were a few people who thought that having a frolic only two days after the murder of a longtime faculty member was just a little bit tacky, but Dean Partridge wasn't one of them.

Her memo on the subject said:

> *Inasmuch as the students will need something to relieve their minds in the current gloomy circumstances, it seems appropriate to continue with the Spring Frolic as scheduled. Samantha Henderson has expressed her personal wish that everything at HGC continue in as routine a fashion as possible.*

The memo reminded Burns of a couple of things. One was that he hated the Spring Frolic and every year tried to avoid as many of its activities as possible. The other was that he still hadn't paid a call on Henderson's wife. He didn't like doing things like that, though he considered it more or less a duty, and he would have to do something about it.

As he sat in his office looking out over the campus, he thought about Tom Henderson and the Spring Frolic. As a matter of fact, Henderson hadn't liked the Frolic any better than Burns did. The two of them had occasionally stood in Henderson's office and watched the yearly Mud Tug, commenting sarcastically on the participants.

Henderson's window looked out not only over the sidewalk where he had fallen to his death but also over the patch of ground where the Mud Tug took place. Burns, who would never have dreamed of taking part, nevertheless wasn't averse to watching others make fools of themselves, especially if two of the potential fools were Tomlin and Fox.

It had always surprised Burns that those two would willingly take part in something like the Mud Tug, which was simply a tug-of-war between the freshmen (or, as they were now called, thanks to Dean Partridge, the first year students) and the faculty, or at least those faculty who were willing to risk being dragged through ten yards of slimy muck.

Early on the morning of the Frolic, the maintenance crew would quite thoroughly wet down the turf in the middle of the patch of ground overlooked by Henderson's window. Then, during the hour scheduled for Assembly, the faculty and first-year students would gather around opposite ends of the thick rope that the maintenance workers had left lying across the sludge they had created earlier. At a signal from the college president, who also had declined to participate more directly, as had been the tradition with HGC presidents from the first right down to the present one, the participants would grab hold of the rope and begin to pull.

The object of the exercise, of course, was for one side to pull the other through the gummy slime, while at the same time relaxing just enough at the end to give the losers hope that they might be able to return the favor. But as soon as the losers got back to more solid footing, the stronger team would always drag them right back into the ooze.

Burns couldn't think of anything he would rather do less than slop around in the mud, but Fox and Tomlin had never seemed to mind. They defended the activity as good for the morale of the students, but Burns told them that while that might be true, getting slimed wouldn't be good for *his* morale.

So there he was, sitting alone in his office in the deserted building while practically everyone else was out to frolic in the mud.

Well, that wasn't exactly true. Miss Darling certainly wasn't going to get into the act, nor was Clem. But they were outside to watch, ready to cheer on the certain-to-be-over-matched faculty. Holt, who preferred afternoon classes, wasn't around yet, and Burns didn't know him well enough to predict whether he would be pulling or cheering had he been there.

Burns stood up and walked around his desk. He couldn't see the Mud Tug from where he was, and while he didn't want to go outside, he would have liked to see if just for once the faculty could win the annual battle.

Maybe Tom Henderson's office would be open.

Burns made his way through the deserted corridors, the old boards beneath the carpet creaking under his feet. He went down the stairs to the second floor.

There was no one there, either, and Burns went on back to Henderson's office.

The office was locked, which was certainly not surprising. And there was a yellow plastic ribbon stretched across the doorway. The ribbon said that this was a line Burns should not cross, but he didn't take the warning seriously. After all, who was going to find out?

The locked door didn't pose any problems. As Burns had reason to know, it was quite easy to slide a credit card between the door and the frame and slip the lock. He pulled out his wallet and extracted his Visa card.

The door to Henderson's office fit the frame a little more tightly than Burns had expected, but he had it open in less than a minute. He replaced his plastic, ducked under the ribbon, and went inside, pulling the door shut behind him.

The office was darker than it would normally have been because the window through which Henderson had crashed was now covered with cardboard held in place with silver duct tape. There was another window, over Henderson's desk, and Burns could see outside without standing too close to it. If anyone happened to look up, Burns wouldn't be seen.

Or if he were seen, he would appear as nothing more than a shadow, the same kind of shadow that Burns had noticed the evening of Henderson's fall.

The Frolic was in full swing down below, and Burns could hear the cheering of the first-year students as well as the faculty.

He risked a peek.

The students were winning the Mud Tug easily, with the faculty forces being drawn inexorably toward the mire. In only a matter of seconds, it would be all over. Fox and Tomlin were near the end of the rope, so they would be the last ones in the mud, but they would be in it nevertheless. Burns smiled to himself.

And then he saw that Elaine Tanner was on the rope.

He stopped smiling.

He suddenly wished he were down there with everyone else, and a brief but entertaining fantasy of mud-wrestling with the librarian raced through his brain.

He shook his head to clear it. If that wasn't sexism, nothing was. Next he would be snorting and oinking and rooting for acorns.

He knew that he hadn't really come to Henderson's office to watch the Frolic and the Mud Tug, anyway. He had come to look around.

He didn't know exactly what he was looking for, true, but whatever it was, it wouldn't be outside. It would be in there with him.

He tore his gaze away from the outdoors, thinking of his visit to Henderson earlier in the semester, trying to remember how the office had looked and what had been in it.

It was just an ordinary office, with bookshelves, two chairs (one for the professor, one for visitors), a desk, and a typing table on which there was an old IBM electric. Most of HGC's faculty hadn't entered the computer era yet. There was a gray plastic dustcover on the typewriter.

Burns lifted the dustcover. There was nothing rolled into the typewriter. No suicide note that the police had overlooked, no forgotten assignment sheet. Burns hadn't really expected that there would be.

He looked at the bookshelves. Plenty of out-of-date psy-

chology textbooks, some biographies, some books of theory.
There was even a book on suicide, but Burns was pretty sure
that meant nothing.

Burns turned toward the desk. He had saved it for last
because he remembered it best. If there were any clues to be
found, they would be there on the desk. He had already
noticed several obvious differences in its appearance.

The desk calendar was still there, though the page hadn't
been turned for today, and there was also an old college
yearbook from Henderson's alma mater lying out in plain
sight. That had certainly not been there on Burns's last visit.
He picked it up and flipped through the pages, looking at the
photos.

He paused when he came to a very young Thomas E.
Henderson. There was no sign of the baldness that had
begun to afflict Henderson in later life. The young man's
hair was long and shaggy, hanging down over his ears. His
face was, if anything, thinner than it had been in later life.

Burns wondered whether Henderson had simply been
engaged in nostalgia for his lost youth or whether he had
been looking at the yearbook for some other reason. A
sudden nostalgia attack seemed unlikely, and Burns began
to pay close attention to the photos of the other students.

There were a lot of pictures, though they represented only
a fraction of the student body. Most people didn't bother to
have photos made.

A loud cheer from outside made Burns look through the
window again. The Mud Tug was over, and now the general
frolicking had begun. First-year students were shoving soph-
omores into the mud, while upperclassmen (or upper-
classpersons, or whatever they were supposed to be called
now—Burns couldn't quite remember) were pushing one
another toward the gooey area lately wallowed in by the
faculty.

Burns couldn't see Elaine, which was probably just as well.
He hoped that she had gone inside.

But now he had to hurry. Everyone would be staying

outside for a few more minutes, and then many of them would be going to get cleaned up. Some of them, however, like Clem and Miss Darling, would be coming back into the buildings.

Burns looked back at the yearbook. There was no one in it whose photo looked familiar. He ran his finger along under the pictures. A lot of young, earnest faces. Maybe Henderson had known them, but Burns didn't.

His finger continued to move. It went past one photo, stopped, slid back.

Henry (Hank) Mitchum. A clean-shaven young man with wide eyes, well-groomed hair, a weak chin.

Burns had never heard of him, but there was something about him that looked familiar. Something about the eyes.

They looked like Eric Holt's eyes.

Burns closed the yearbook and looked back at the desk. There was something else there that hadn't been there before.

An HGC recruiting brochure.

Burns stuck the yearbook under his left arm and reached for the brochure with his right hand.

Just as he touched it, someone rattled the doorknob.

Burns jerked his hand back, thinking of being caught by the police inside an office where he wasn't supposed to be. He looked for a place to hide, but of course there wasn't any such place, unless he ducked into the kneehole of the desk. That might hide him for about two seconds.

The doorknob rattled again, harder this time, and Burns realized that the police wouldn't rattle the knob. They would simply use the key and unlock the door. Whoever was trying to get in had no more right to be there than Burns did.

Panic turned to curiosity. Burns decided to help out whoever was trying to get in by opening the door, but as he reached for the knob the yearbook slid from under his arm. It struck the carpeted floor with a dull thump.

There was a moment of silence. Then Burns heard footsteps thudding down the hallway outside the door.

He jerked open the door and charged out, ripping away the police ribbon in the process. He wondered what Boss Napier would do to him for that. Probably nothing, since Burns made an instantaneous decision not to tell the police chief who had done it. He pulled the ribbon away from his waist and threw it to the floor as he ran down the hallway.

The person who had rattled the doorknob was no longer in sight, having turned the corner at the end of the hall. Burns was no track star, but he thought he might be able to catch up.

When he reached the head of the stairs, he could hear footsteps on the bare first floor. He was going to have to hurry to get even a glimpse.

He might have made it had he not hooked a toe in the frayed carpeting and pitched headfirst down the stairs.

He hit the stairs halfway down, had the presence of mind to tuck his head, and did a complete flip, touching down this time on his tailbone and bouncing forward over the last two steps to the landing where the stairway turned to go on down to the first floor.

Burns sat very still for a while, trying to decide which was hurting worse, his tailbone or his pride. Other parts of him hurt as well: his shoulders, his neck, and his back.

He was sure he must have been quite a sight during his pratfall, at least as funny as the Mud Tuggers and maybe even funnier. He was extremely thankful that there had been no one there to see him take the plunge, though whoever had rattled the doorknob had probably heard him whumpty-whumping down the stairway.

After a minute or so, Burns tried to get up. It wasn't easy, but by bracing himself on the wall and pushing with his hands, he was able to stand. He didn't feel any better in that position, and rather than risk walking he simply stood there for another minute.

There was still no one in the building. There was that to be grateful for. He wondered if he had broken any important bones. It was bad enough that he had recently broken his nose and had to go around looking like the Masked Avenger. This would be even worse.

He took a few deep breaths and decided it was about time to try going back upstairs.

The first step was the hardest. After that, he just kept going. It wasn't so bad. A little like having a spear jabbed into your lower backbone with every step. He thought about what it was going to be like to sit down. It wasn't a very pleasant thought.

On the positive side, there didn't seem to be any bones grinding together in ways that they shouldn't have. Maybe nothing was broken.

It took Burns several minutes to get back to Henderson's office. He wasn't going to bother replacing the police ribbon, but he was going to pick up the yearbook and the recruiting brochure, both of which he wanted to think about a little longer.

Neither was proof of anything, but the brochure was suggestive. It was the kind of thing that Walt Melling might have been carrying, might even have dropped in the office. If the police had seen it on the floor, they might have assumed that it was knocked off the desk and replaced it there.

The yearbook was suggestive, too. There was nothing out of the ordinary about a yearbook in a professor's office. Burns had several yearbooks in his own office, both from his student days and his more recent years at HGC. But he didn't look at them often, and he was sure that Henderson had gotten this one out and looked at it for a good reason. Henry Mitchum's photo would bear closer examination.

And there was one other thing.

Something that *wasn't* there.

It was a little like the dog in the Sherlock Holmes story, the dog that didn't bark.

▽

11

BY THE TIME he went home that afternoon, Burns's tailbone wasn't hurting quite as much as it had been. He was even able to sit in his car without shrieking aloud when he touched the seat. It wasn't very pleasant to hit even the smallest of Pecan City's chuckholes as he drove along, however.

He spent some of his time at home debating about whether to call Elaine Tanner and ask her to visit Samantha Henderson with him. He finally decided that she wouldn't hold his association with George (The Ghost) Kaspar against him and punched in the librarian's number on his phone.

"I don't think I know her," she said, when he told her what he wanted.

He'd been afraid she might say something like that. She hadn't been at HGC long enough to meet everyone.

"I don't like to go alone," he told her. "I never know what to say."

"All right, then. I'll go."

She didn't sound enthusiastic about it, but Burns didn't care. He was just glad to have company for the visit, especially Elaine's company.

"Thanks," he said. He paused. "I saw you at the Mud Tug this afternoon."

"I didn't see you. Earl and Mal told me you thought you were too good to roll in the mud."

"It's not that." He thought about his sore tailbone. "It's just that I have an injury."

"What kind of injury?" She sounded skeptical.

"It's . . . an old baseball injury. My back. It acts up now and then, but I hardly ever mention it. I don't like to use it as an excuse."

"Your back?" She didn't sound exactly convinced, but he could tell she was weakening.

"Yes." Burns felt inspired. He could almost hear the crack of the bat against the old horsehide. "I hurt it turning a double play."

"You played the infield?"

"That's right. Second base." That much was true. It was Little League ball, but he had been a second baseman. "The ball took a bad hop, so I had to twist around to make the throw to the shortstop. I felt something pop, but we got the two."

"You'll have to tell me more about your baseball career someday."

"Sure," Burns said, wondering where he could get his hands on a book that would have some good baseball stories in it. "Maybe we could take in one of the college's games."

Elaine wasn't going to let him off the hook about George that easily. "Maybe."

"Maybe" was better than nothing. Burns was feeling a little better when he hung up.

Samantha Henderson lived in an older section of town known as the Heights, for reasons that might have been clear to an earlier generation of Pecan City inhabitants but that made no sense at all to Burns. Unless, of course, you considered an elevation of maybe thirty feet a "height." The homes in the Heights were mostly frame houses shaded by oak trees and surrounded by green lawns.

Samantha Henderson lived in the middle of a block, and Burns parked his gigantic old Plymouth at the curb. He stepped out on the cracked sidewalk and waited for Elaine to join him. The thought of going around the car to open the door for her had entered his mind, but he had quickly

rejected it. He didn't want her to think he was an old-fashioned dweeb.

It was nearly dark, but Burns could see no lights on in the
Henderson house as he hobbled up the walk.

Elaine pretended not to notice the hitch in his stride. "Do
you think she's home?"

"Where else would she be?"

"At the funeral home."

"The visitation was yesterday," Burns said.

Visitation was another custom he wasn't in favor of. He
knew that he should go to the funeral home to show his
support for the family, but he didn't like the idea of sitting
around talking cheerfully in the presence of a corpse. It
wasn't so bad if the casket was closed, but that usually
wasn't the case. So, offered a choice between visiting the
family at home or at the funeral parlor, Burns chose the
home.

They reached the door, and Burns rang the bell. There was
no response for what seemed like a long time. Then Burns
heard the sound of a dead bolt being thrown, and the door
opened.

Samantha Henderson looked terrible. There were dark
circles underneath her eyes, her hair was uncombed, and
she was wearing a dress that looked as if she might have
slept in it.

Burns knew that he was guilty of looksism, but he
couldn't help it. Even Elaine looked somewhat shocked.

"Oh," Samantha said. Her voice was not much more than
a whisper. "Hello, Dr. Burns."

"Hello, Samantha," Burns said. "This is Elaine Tanner.
She's the school librarian. You may have met her at school."

"Hello, Miss Tanner. It was nice of you to come."

Burns thought that she couldn't have sounded less enthusiastic had Dracula himself, or maybe the Wolfman, been
standing outside her door. He waited for her to invite them
in, but she said nothing further. They all stood there
awkwardly.

Finally Burns said, "Could we come in for a minute?"

Samantha stepped back. "Of course."

She turned and walked in front of them to the living room. All the curtains were drawn, and the room was so dark that Burns could hardly make out the furniture.

"I suppose I should turn on a light," Samantha said, but she made no move to do so.

"A light might be a good idea," Burns said.

"Yes," Elaine said, walking over to a floor lamp and switching it on when Samantha made no move to do so.

The light didn't help the room. It appeared that Samantha had done no cleaning since Tom's death. In fact, it appeared that she hadn't done any cleaning for a long time before that. Magazines lay on the floor by an overstuffed chair, that seemed to be leaning slightly to the left as if its springs were broken. There was a thin layer of dust on the coffee table, and there was a faint odor of decay that Burns couldn't identify.

"Please have a seat," Samantha said.

Burns looked at Elaine, who went directly to the couch and sat down. Burns joined her. A sharp pain ran up his back when he sat, but he was a former athlete. It wasn't anything he couldn't deal with. Samantha continued to stand. She wasn't looking at her guests. She was looking out one of the living room windows, though there was nothing to see.

"We were certainly sorry about Tom's death," Burns said. It was the only thing he could think of.

"Thank you," Samantha said. She was still looking out the window. "I miss him very much."

There was another awkward pause while Burns tried to think of something else to say. Elaine wasn't any help at all.

"They told me he was murdered," Samantha said, her voice growing a little stronger. "But I don't believe it."

It was the last thing Burns would have expected her to say, but since she had brought it up herself, he thought it was worth pursuing.

"Why not?" he asked.

Samantha turned and looked at him. "Everyone loved Tom. Who would have killed him?"

"That's what I've been wondering," Burns said. Elaine jabbed him with an elbow, but he paid her no attention.

"It might have been that horrible Mal Tomlin," Samantha said.

Burns sat up a little straighter, ignoring the twinge in his tailbone. "Who?

"Mal Tomlin. You must know who he is."

"I know him," Burns said. "Why would he kill Tom?"

"He was jealous of him. Mal's wife was very attracted to Tom."

Burns thought of Joynell Tomlin, a cheerful blond who liked to think of herself as resembling Dolly Parton, though the truth was that she was more likely to be the winner in a Pillsbury Doughboy look-alike contest. As far as Burns knew, she was completely faithful to Mal.

"Or maybe it was Earl Fox."

"Earl Fox?"

"Of course. His wife made several advances toward Tom."

This had to be one of the most bizarre conversations of Burns's life. Rae Fox was a tall, thin brunette with a tan that rivaled George Hamilton's. Earl sometimes joked that if she died before he did, he was going to make seat covers for his car from her skin. He didn't make the joke in front of Rae, however. Burns would have bet a year's salary that Rae Fox had never looked at Tom Henderson with anything resembling interest.

"That was Tom's trouble, you know," Samantha said.

"What was?"

"What I said before. Everyone loved him. Especially the women. The women loved him so much that it got him killed."

Burns wondered if she knew about Dawn Melling, but he thought it would be better not to mention it. She seemed to have enough candidates for her husband's murderer already.

"Did you tell the police what you suspect?" he asked.

"Yes. I didn't see any need to protect those men. If they're guilty, they should be punished."

"That's true," Burns said, though he didn't think that either of the two men she had mentioned had anything to do with Henderson's death. Convincing Boss Napier, however, might be another story. He might be very willing to believe Samantha Henderson.

"The funeral is tomorrow, you know," Samantha said.

"Yes," Burns told her. "We know. We'll be there."

"That will be nice," Samantha said.

Burns got up. He thought he'd brought about as much comfort into Samantha Henderson's home as he possibly could. Elaine got up and stood beside him.

"We'll have to be going now," Burns said.

"It was nice of you to come by. You, too, Miss Tanner."

"We're so sorry about Tom," Elaine said, and Samantha started to cry.

"That was interesting," Elaine said when they were in Burns's car.

"It certainly was. Did you believe any of it?"

Elaine was stony-faced. "I don't know the people involved well enough to believe or disbelieve anything."

Burns wondered about her tone. Then he had a thought. "Did you ever talk much to Tom?"

Elaine half-turned to look at him. "What do you mean by that?"

"I think you know."

"All right. I did talk to him once. He came to the library to ask me about ordering a book."

"He came to your office?"

"That's right. And there was no one else there, if that's your next question, Mr. Private Detective."

"Wait a minute," Burns said. "You're the one who was going on to Boss Napier about my being one of his ace investigators." He had another thought. "You didn't tell Napier about Henderson's visit to your office, did you?"

"Why should I?"

"Because he made a pass at you, didn't he?"

" 'Made a pass.' That's such old-fashioned language."

"You're avoiding the question," Burns pointed out.

"All right. Maybe I am. But he didn't make a pass, as you put it. Not exactly. It wasn't so much what he said as the way he said it."

Remembering what Henderson had said to Dawn, Burns wondered if the late professor had said something similar to Elaine. He didn't think it would be a good idea to ask, however. So he just waited to see if Elaine would go on.

"That's why I was a little hesitant about coming with you tonight," she said. "Because of that little incident."

"What about Samantha's idea that Joynell and Ræ were coming on to Tom?"

"That was projection on Tom's part if he told his wife that," Elaine said. "I'm sure that if anything happened, the women weren't responsible. Doesn't that help you to see how insidious sexism can be?"

"I don't have any trouble seeing that. But I think it's wrong to hold all men responsible for the acts of a creep like Tom Henderson. I don't believe that most men are like that."

"Only because you're not."

Burns tried to leer. "Maybe I am."

Elaine smiled. "No, you're not. I wouldn't be here if you were."

"I guess that's a compliment. And since you're so sure I'm harmless, if we go by my house, would you come in and look at something?"

"What? Your etchings?"

"I don't have any etchings. I'm not even sure what etchings are."

"Good. So what do you want me to look at?"

"It's a surprise," Burns said.

"All right," Elaine said.

*　*　*

Burns didn't have any wine, and he didn't have any designer water, so he asked Elaine if she would like some Pepsi. She said that would be fine.

"What did you have to show me?" she asked when he had poured the soft drink.

Burns went into his office and brought out the yearbook he had found in Henderson's office. He had spent part of the afternoon examining the picture of Henry Mitchum with a magnifying glass. He still couldn't make up his mind about it.

"I didn't know you went to San Diego State," Elaine said when she saw the cover of the yearbook. "Did you play baseball there?"

"No," Burns said. "That was somewhere else. This yearbook isn't mine. It belonged to Tom Henderson."

"How did you get it?"

"I don't think you want to know."

"Why not?"

"Never mind. I want you to look at some pictures."

Burns opened the book to the page with Mitchum's photo. He handed the book to Elaine.

"What am I supposed to be looking for?"

"I can't tell you that. Well, maybe I can. I want you to tell me if anyone on those two pages looks familiar."

Elaine set her Pepsi on the coffee table and took the yearbook. She held it in her lap and looked down at the photographs. Burns sat beside her, ignoring the pain in his backside, and waited patiently for her to say something.

"Maybe this one does," she said after several minutes.

She had her finger under the picture of Henry Mitchum.

"Why?" Burns asked.

"I'm not sure. Something about the eyes."

Burns decided to give her a hint. "Think about the HGC faculty."

Elaine thought. And thought.

"The English faculty," Burns said.

Elaine thought some more. Then she said, "Eric Holt?"

Bingo, Burns thought. "That's what I thought. But it's hard to say for sure."

"What difference does it make if two men happen to resemble one another."

Burns explained that Henderson thought he recognized Holt from somewhere and that the yearbook had been on Henderson's desk.

"I'm not sure I see what you're getting at," Elaine said.

"I was just wondering if Eric Holt is really who he says he is," Burns said.

He went on to explain that Holt was, after all, a somewhat mysterious character, a well-published scholar who never went to meetings and preferred to spend his life as far from the academic mainstream as he could get.

"But this probably isn't even him," Elaine said. "It's only something about the eyes. What about the rest of the face?"

"Holt has that thick beard. The eyes are the only thing we have to go on."

"It's not a lot."

Burns had to admit that it wasn't. "And even if it does mean something, it doesn't prove that Holt had anything to do with Henderson's death."

"So what are you going to do?"

"I'm going to see if I can find out anything about this Henry Mitchum. I'll call the school tomorrow." Burns took the yearbook from Elaine. "And I'd appreciate it if you didn't say anything about this to Boss Napier. This is probably nothing at all, and I wouldn't want to get Holt into any unnecessary trouble."

"Do you think R.M. might do something to Eric?"

Burns didn't like to hear Elaine using Holt's first name any more than he liked hearing her refer to "R.M."

"No. Well, he might question him. I don't want to start anything like that until I have more to go on."

"What about your friends?"

"What friends?"

"You know very well. Mal and Earl. You heard what Mrs.

Henderson said about them, and she said that she told R.M. the same thing."

Burns admitted that he was a little worried. "But I'm sure they didn't do anything to Henderson, because I'm sure their wives are completely innocent. If anything happened between them and Henderson, they dealt with it themselves, just as you did, and didn't tell anyone."

"Maybe they told each other."

Burns thought that was likely, but he was more interested in something else. "Just exactly what did Henderson say to you that day in the library, by the way?"

"He said something about my figure."

"And what did you tell him?"

"I told him that if he didn't get out of my office in two seconds I was going to stuff a bull-riding trophy down his throat."

"And did he leave?"

"Of course he did. He could tell I wasn't kidding."

Burns thought about that. "I guess I shouldn't try making a pass at you then, should I?"

Elaine looked around the room. "Oh, I don't know. I don't see any trophies handy."

Burns smiled. This was turning out to be quite a night.

$\triangledown$

12

Burns was feeling awfully good the next day, better than he'd felt in a long time. Thanks to his mildly successful pass of the previous evening, he was beginning to think that maybe he was getting a little bit ahead of Boss Napier in the race for Elaine's affections.

He didn't want to think about murder at all, but now that he'd started investigating, he couldn't stop. There was something about digging into people's secrets and their pasts that he couldn't resist. Maybe he really did have a talent for investigation.

He could hardly wait to get to the boiler room and talk to Fox and Tomlin.

Fox and Tomlin, on the other hand, were not nearly so pleased with what was going on in their lives. It seemed that Boss Napier had already made his first move in their direction. Burns was actually somewhat grateful; Napier's machinations kept their minds off the fact that Burns hadn't showed up for the Mud Tug.

"I want to know what the hell's going on, Burns," Tomlin said, sucking on his Merit and then breathing out a cloud of smoke. "You've got an in with that cop. What's he questioning our wives about?"

"Hasn't your wife told you?" Burns asked, suddenly craving a cigarette himself. He controlled the impulse to ask for one, however.

"She hasn't talked to him yet. She's supposed to go in this morning."

"Rae's going in, too," Fox said, lighting a Cost Cutter. Smoke spiraled lazily up toward the thirty-foot ceiling of the boiler room. "I don't understand what's going on."

Burns enlightened them. "I talked to Samantha Henderson last night. She has this fantasy about your wives having been in love with her husband. And maybe one of you killed him in a rit of fellous jage."

"That's from one of those Pink Panther movies," Tomlin said. "And I don't think it's a damn bit funny. Joynell wouldn't have given that creep Henderson a second look, so I didn't have anything to be jealous of."

"And Rae thought he was a weirdo," Fox said, as if that settled everything.

"I didn't mean to make a joke of it," Burns said. "Napier's convinced that Henderson was murdered, and he has to check every lead."

"He'd better not use that bullwhip on Joynell," Tomlin told them. "That's all I can say."

"Do you think we'll be questioned?" Fox asked.

It was clear that he viewed getting called to the police station as an evil even worse than getting caught smoking on campus. Or maybe it was the thought of the bullwhip that scared him.

"I don't see why," Burns said. "After Napier talks to your wives, he'll know you're in the clear."

"He'd better," Tomlin said. He dropped the butt of his Merit to the concrete floor and stepped on it, twisting his foot viciously.

Burns was holding the yearbook. After telling them where he had found it, he showed them the picture of Henry Mitchum.

"It's that damn Holt," Tomlin said almost at once. "I knew it! He's living under an assumed name because he did some crime back in California. He was Mitchum then, but he's Holt now, and he killed Henderson!"

"That's a pretty big logical leap," Burns said.

Tomlin clearly didn't think so. "The hell it is. Nobody changes his name for nothing."

"We don't know that Holt is Mitchum," Burns reminded him.

"Look at those eyes. I bet Holt knew that Henderson was checking up on him. Maybe he even knew about this yearbook. He was probably going after it when he killed Tom."

"It was on Tom's desk," Burns said. "No one took it."

"Panic," Earl Fox said, dropping one Cost Cutter and getting another out of the pack. "He ran away without it after he knocked Tom through the window."

"Right," Tomlin said. "I knew it all along. Damn hippies. Tom saw him on 'America's Most Wanted,' I'll bet you anything."

"He had the yearbook," Burns said. "He didn't need to see anyone on television."

Tomlin ignored him. "And what's more, there's some connection between Holt and Partridge. That's why he's here, and you can mark my words. The two of them probably offed Henderson."

"Offed?" Burns said. "*Offed?*"

"Right. They offed him. Now all we have to do is catch them together."

"What would that prove?" Burns asked.

"You're the detective," Tomlin said. "You figure it out."

Burns tried, but he didn't see the connection. He had, however, thought of a better way to get information on Henry Mitchum than by calling the school. He would get Napier to check to see if Mitchum had a criminal record. He told Fox and Tomlin his plan.

"Maybe you ought to talk to Holt first," Fox said. "Hear his side of this."

Tomlin snorted smoke through his nose. "Yeah. Right. If he *has* a side."

"No, Earl's right," Burns said. "I do have to talk to Eric."

But not about the photo, he thought. No need to make Holt any more suspicious than he was likely to be when Burns asked him about his whereabouts on Tuesday evening.

Besides, it was possible that Henderson had said something to Holt about the picture, and look where Henderson was now.

That thought reminded Burns of something. "Are you two going to the funeral tomorrow?"

"Sure," Tomlin said. "But only because I feel like I have to."

Burns knew what he meant.

"What about you, Earl?"

"Yes. That is, if Rae doesn't have other plans for us. It was thoughtful of Samantha to wait till Saturday for the burial, wasn't it? That way it won't interfere with classes."

"You could go without Rae," Tomlin said.

"I could, but I'm not."

Burns decided to head off what appeared to be an argument. "I have something else I need to know, Earl."

"What's that?"

"The name of that student who complained to you about Henderson."

"I told you I didn't think I could give you her name."

"It's a murder case now," Burns reminded him. "Would you rather have me or Boss Napier talk to the student?"

"Well, since you put it that way . . ."

"I don't want to hear this," Tomlin said. "I'm not a detective." He threw his cigarette to the floor. "I'll see you guys later."

When Tomlin was out the door, Burns said, "Her name, Earl?"

"Kristi Albert. Kristi with a 'K.' And with an 'i' on the end."

"Thanks," Burns said. "I'll keep this confidential."

"Just get me off the hook with Napier. That's all I ask."

"I'll do what I can," Burns promised, though he wasn't sure he could do anything at all.

Next Burns wanted to talk to Walt Melling. He went to the recruiting office, hoping that Melling was in. When he had

an especially long recruiting trip on the weekend, he sometimes left before noon on Friday.

However, the former football player was sitting at his desk
when Burns walked in. Burns sat down, which was not so
painful today, made small talk for a few seconds, and then
reached inside his jacket for the recruiting brochure he had
picked up in Henderson's office.

"What's that?" Melling asked.

Burns laid it on the desk. "You've seen a lot of them, I'm
sure."

Everyone knew that Melling was never without a handful
of the colorful blue-and-white pamphlets stuffed into his
jacket pockets.

"Have I ever," Melling said. "What's so special about this
one?"

"There's nothing special about the brochure," Burns said.
"But there's something special about where it was found."

Melling was suddenly wary. "What's that to me?"

"It was found in Tom Henderson's office." Burns hoped
the passive voice might imply that the police had found the
brochure instead of him.

Melling leaned back in his chair. "Big deal. There are
thousands of these things all over this campus."

"This one has your fingerprints all over it," Burns said, a
blatant lie, since Burns hadn't the least idea about how
fingerprints were obtained. And if there had been any of
Melling's fingerprints on the brochure, they were probably
gone by now. Burns had been handling the thing himself for
hours before even thinking about the possibility of fingerprints.

"So what? I've touched nearly all of those pamphlets at
one time or another."

"The way we put it together," Burns said, using the royal
"we" and hoping it would mislead Melling into thinking that
Burns had already discussed things with the police, "you
were in Tom's office on the afternoon he was killed. You
probably dropped this brochure then."

Melling patted his jacket pockets, pulled out a recruiting pamphlet, and showed it to Burns. "I carry these things everywhere. I could have dropped it anytime. And besides, I'm not the only one who carries recruiting brochures around, you know."

"I know," Burns said. "But the third floor isn't on any of the recruiting schedules that I've seen, and you're the only one who might have had a reason to be in Henderson's office." He held up his own pamphlet. "And this one has your fingerprints on it."

Melling put the pamphlet he was holding back in his pocket. Then he sat forward and leaned his forearms on his desk. "All right, Burns. So I was in Henderson's office. Big deal. What's the harm with going by and talking to someone?"

"You told me that you were here at your desk when Henderson fell."

"That's exactly where I was. I was working on some expense sheets."

"So you couldn't have killed him."

Melling moved his hands from the top of the desk and held them out of Burns's sight. Burns imagined them balling into hard fists.

"That's right," Melling said. "I didn't kill him. I wanted to smash his wormy little face in. He deserved it, but I didn't do that, either."

Melling was lying, and Burns knew it. He couldn't explain how he knew, but he was certain of it. Something in Melling's tone of voice gave him away, that and the rapid reddening of his face. Napier had told Burns and Elaine that Henderson had been struck in the face before his fall. Burns was sure that Melling was the one who had hit him.

"Why didn't you hit him?" Burns asked, deciding to take a chance on getting his own wormy face smashed in. "After all, he said something about your wife's breasts, didn't he? Let's see, how did he put it?"

Burns didn't get a chance to say how Henderson had put

it because Melling stood up, reached for Burns, grabbed his jacket, and pulled him halfway across the desk.

"I told you," Melling said, his face purple. "People shouldn't say things like that. And you shouldn't repeat them, either."

He shoved Burns back into the chair, and this time Burns's tailbone gave a healthy twinge.

"You should have a checkup, Walt," Burns said. "Your color's bad. You probably have high blood pressure."

"Don't you talk about my blood pressure, you little . . . insect."

Burns didn't know whether being an insect was better than being a worm. "Walt, I think you should talk to me about what happened in Tom's office."

Melling was breathing hard. "I've told you all I have to tell. And you can go squealing to the cops if you want to. I don't give a damn. Now get out of here."

Burns thought about prolonging the conversation, but it would look bad if one of the suspects had a stroke before anything was proved against him. So Burns started to leave quietly.

Melling was still standing behind his desk, his fists resting on top. His face wasn't quite so purple now, and he was getting his breathing under control.

It was sad to see a former athlete go to seed like that, and Burns, the old second baseman, vowed not to let it happen to him.

"Wait a second," Melling said, just as Burns stepped through the door.

Burns turned around. Melling didn't look quite so malevolent now.

"There's one thing I forgot," Melling said.

Burns stood in the doorway, but he didn't reenter the office. "What's that?"

"I saw somebody that afternoon. Just as I was leaving Henderson's office."

"Who?" Burns asked.

"I don't know her, but I'm sure she's a student. I've seen her on campus." Melling went on to describe a woman who seemed to look a lot like the one Burns had seen fleeing Henderson's office in tears. "She's the one you should be talking to," Melling concluded. "Not me."

"You could be right about that," Burns said.

But he wasn't convinced. Maybe Melling had actually seen someone, but he could have seen her before going to Henderson's office. Or maybe he hadn't seen her at all. Maybe he'd heard about Kristi Albert and decided to use her to his advantage. Nevertheless, it was one more thing Burns would have to check out as soon as he got a chance. There were a couple of other things he wanted to do first.

That afternoon Burns went around to talk to Eric Holt, hoping that he would have better luck than he'd had with Melling. He couldn't have any worse, that was for sure.

He was going to have to talk to Napier again soon, too. It was time to put the police chief in the picture about what was really going on before he wasted too much time questioning people like Joynell and Rae. Walt Melling was a much more likely suspect than Mal Tomlin or Earl Fox.

And then there was Holt. Things just weren't right there, though it was hard to say what was wrong. Burns remembered something Dean Partridge had told him and Napier: "Dr. Henderson's death has nothing to do with the past." Burns wasn't sure that was true, and he still hadn't found out all he wanted to know about Holt's past.

The third floor of Main was practically deserted. On Friday afternoons, there was generally no one there except Holt. Burns, like the rest of the faculty, believed that Friday afternoons were not created for staying on campus, and he was there only to catch Holt alone.

Holt was in his office, watching an old Republic serial on the video monitor that he had on permanent loan from Student Services. Burns was lucky if he could get a monitor to show snippets from the two most recent film versions of

The Great Gatsby to his classes, but Holt had Dean Partridge to go to bat for him. Therefore he got to have a VCR and monitor in his office.

Burns recognized the serial; it was *The Masked Marvel*, not one of his favorites, but still worth watching.

"Some pretty good stunt work in that one," he said from Holt's open doorway.

Holt froze the picture and turned to see who was there. "Good afternoon, Dr. Burns. Do you know about Tom Steele?"

"He was the Masked Marvel, but he didn't get any screen credit. Doubled some stunts for the bad guys, too, didn't he?"

Holt was as impressed as someone else might have been had Burns been able to recite a passage from *Antigone* in classical Greek. "That's right. You know your serials, Dr. Burns."

"Some of them, anyway," Burns said. "Mind if I come in?"

"Please do. We can watch chapter eight."

"I don't really have time for that. I wanted to talk to you about something else."

"All right." Holt turned off the VCR and monitor. "What did you have in mind?"

"I guess you've heard about Tom Henderson."

Holt looked concerned. "Yes. Terrible thing. Just terrible. I'm sure the students were greatly affected. It was an excellent idea for Dean Partridge to set up grief counseling for them."

Burns, who didn't want to talk about grief counseling, studied Holt's face, trying to get some idea of what the chin would be like without the beard. It was impossible to tell. The eyes were right, though.

"Yes," he said. "But I'm sure it was harder on you than on most of the students."

Holt, who had been leaning back in his chair, sat up a little straighter. "What? Why?"

"Well, I had the impression that you and Henderson knew

one another from way back. Weren't you in college together?"

"Of course not. Whatever gave you that idea?"

Burns shrugged. "Something Tom said one day. About your looking like someone he knew in school. He seemed pretty sure he remembered you."

"Impossible. I don't recall ever having seen him before coming to HGC."

"Maybe I heard wrong. You didn't go to school in California?"

"No. I went to North Texas State, as it was called in those days. I've never even *been* to California."

Burns wondered why Holt was so insistent. "So there's no way you could have known Henderson?"

Holt shook his magnificent head. "I don't see how."

"There was someone else that Tom mentioned. Henry Mitchum. Sometimes called Hank. Did you ever know him?"

Holt's mouth didn't fall open, but it was a near thing. "Wh-who?"

"Henry Mitchum," Burns repeated.

"Oh," Holt said, making a quick recovery. "I thought you said *Robert* Mitchum." He laughed weakly. "I hope you don't think I'm old enough to have gone to school with *him*."

"I don't think he went to college," Burns said.

"You're right. He didn't. I guess I couldn't have known him, then, could I?"

"We weren't really talking about Robert, though," Burns said. "We were talking about Henry. Or Hank."

"Afraid I can't help you there, either. Never heard of the fellow. Who is he, anyway?"

"Just someone Tom Henderson mentioned to me. I thought you might have known him."

"Sorry. I didn't."

"That's all right," Burns said. "He was just someone Tom happened to mention. Someone he went to school with." Burns looked at his watch. "Well, I guess I'd better let you get back to your serial."

Burns stepped out the door, walked a pace or two, then turned back in his best Columbo style. "Oh, there was one other thing I wanted to ask."

Holt said, "What?"

"The night Tom was killed. Where were you?"

Holt didn't answer for a few seconds. "I was in my classroom, I suppose. I have a class on Tuesday evenings."

Burns was well aware of that. "So you were questioned by the police?"

"Uh, no. No, I wasn't questioned."

"But I thought they questioned everyone in the building."

"I . . . that was *Tuesday* evening, wasn't it?"

Burns was nothing if not patient. "Yes. Tuesday."

"*Last* Tuesday," Holt said, clearly stalling for time.

"That's right," Burns agreed, giving Holt all the rope he needed. "*Last* Tuesday."

"Um. Let me see. I think I was a little late to class that evening. Yes. That's it. I was late. By the time I got here, there were people swarming all over the building. I asked someone what the trouble was, and I was told that classes had been dismissed because of an accident. I went back to my apartment and read."

Burns didn't say a word. He just stood there, waiting.

"I know that was wrong," Holt said after a second or two. "I can see why you're concerned. You're the chairman, after all. I should have come into the building and checked on my students, but I assumed that they had all gone or were told the same thing I was told."

Burns didn't say a word.

"Of course you're wondering where I was. That's only natural. I know that you stress being in class on time."

Holt was talking too much, and he didn't even know what he was talking about. Burns didn't stress being in class on time. The HGC administration did enough of that without Burns having to say anything.

"I was with Dean Partridge," Holt went on. "She called me in for a conference to discuss how I was getting on. We were talking and lost track of the time. So I was a little late for class."

Burns thought it was time for him to say something. "That's understandable."

"Yes. Yes, it is. And of course it was on her own time. She didn't have a chance to meet with me during regular school hours, so she called me in after five. I thought it would be rude of me to call her attention to the time since she'd made a special effort to meet with me then."

And Burns was sure that Dean Partridge would back Holt up about the meeting if she were ever questioned. So why did he think that it had never taken place?

Maybe because Eric Holt was actually sweating, though it was quite cool in the office. For once, Main's erratic air-conditioning system was functioning perfectly, but Holt's forehead was damp, and a thin trickle of sweat ran down from Holt's hair past the corner of his eye.

"Dean Partridge is pretty considerate, all right," Burns said. "I don't blame you for not mentioning that you were going to be a little late to class. Don't worry about it."

"I won't," Holt said, looking more worried than ever.

Burns left him that way, wondering why he felt so good about having made Holt feel so miserable. He also wondered which man looked guiltier, Holt or Melling. He decided it was a toss-up, though Melling was certainly the more dangerously physical of the two. The recruiter didn't sweat. He turned red and made fists. However, you could never tell about something like that. Holt might react violently if he were pushed or prodded in the right way.

Burns was whistling "Smoke Gets in Your Eyes" when he walked into his office, but he broke off the tune abruptly when he saw who was waiting for him there.

George (The Ghost) Kaspar didn't look happy.

13

GEORGE WAS NO happier than he looked.

"I saw your light on," he said, "so I stopped by. I didn't really think you'd be here this late."

"I had a few things to do," Burns said. "What can I do for you, George?"

"It's probably too late for anybody to do anything," George said. "If you'd just never taught that poem, I wouldn't be in this mess."

Burns sat behind his desk. "Did Ms. Tanner talk to Bunni today?"

George nodded. "For all the good *that* did."

Burns had hoped that Elaine would switch sides, especially after last night. Evidently she hadn't.

"And that's not all," George said.

Burns didn't like the sound of that. "What do you mean?"

"Ms. Tanner told Bunni that looksism is everywhere. She said someone was guilty of it with her."

Burns held in his groan. "Did she say who it was?"

"Don't worry," George said. "It's not you."

He sounded disappointed, Burns thought, not feeling the least relieved. In fact, he dreaded asking his next question. "Did she say who it was?"

"Sure. It's that cop. Boss Napier."

Burns felt the bottom fall out of his stomach. There was only one thing worse than being accused of looksism himself, and this was it. It was worse because he knew exactly whom Boss Napier was going to blame.

No matter that there wasn't any justice in it. Napier would blame Burns.

"Are you sure about this, George?"

"Sure, I'm sure. I talked to Bunni about it. She was thrilled to see that Ms. Tanner was a victim, too. It just strengthens her case, she says."

"How's the rest of the campus taking this?" Burns asked, hoping to distract himself from the issue of Boss Napier's looksism.

George brightened, though not much. "Well, there are a lot of people on my side. And not all of them are guys."

"That's encouraging," Burns said.

"Yeah, but there are a lot of people who *aren't* on my side, too."

"What about the student court?"

"They've set a hearing. It'll be on Monday."

"Monday?" Burns was a bit surprised. "That seems a little too soon for them to have gathered all the facts."

"That's what I thought. But I heard it's Dean Partridge's idea."

That made sense, Burns thought. The dean wanted to get things out in the open and dealt with before too much pressure built up. There would be parents calling, wondering what was going on, and the local newspaper might get hold of the story. No telling where it might go after that; it might even get on the wire services. Dr. Miller wouldn't like the negative publicity that could result. He wouldn't like it at all.

"What I was wondering," George said, "was whether you'd be sort of my defense attorney."

That was all Burns needed. But he couldn't turn George down. So he said, "I'd be glad to, George," even though he didn't mean it. Maybe little white lies didn't count against you too much.

George didn't smile, but he looked a little less glum. "Thanks, Dr. Burns. I didn't really mean it about this being all your fault. It's my fault, and I know it. I shouldn't have let appearances influence my affections."

"Where did you get that idea?" Burns asked.

"I guess I heard it from Bunni."

It figured. "Well, don't worry about it," Burns said. "I don't think this will amount to a thing."

"It might. The student court could ask the school to suspend me. My parents would never forgive me if that happened."

"The court won't do anything like that. I promise."

"Really?" George sounded more hopeful than he had so far. "You think they won't?"

Burns had a sudden flash of himself as Al Pacino at the end of *Scent of a Woman*, pounding the table with his cane and screaming that he'd take a flamethrower to the place. It was a nice picture, but it would never work. He was no Al Pacino. He was more like Jimmy Durante.

"I know they won't," he lied. "You don't have a thing to worry about. I'm a great defense attorney. Taught Perry Mason all he knows."

"That's great." George stood up and stuck out his hand. "I knew I could count on you, Dr. Burns. Thanks."

Burns took the offered hand and shook it. He only wished he had as much faith in himself as George did.

After George left, Burns looked around his office to see if there was anything he needed to take home for the weekend. There was nothing, and he was just about to close the door when the phone rang.

Burns glanced at his watch. Four o'clock. He couldn't remember the last time he'd been in his office at that hour on a Friday afternoon. Who could be calling?

The phone rang again.

Maybe it was Holt. He knew Burns was in. Or maybe it was Elaine. Burns hadn't had time to talk to her all day. She might be lonely. It was a nice thought.

The phone rang again, echoing down the deserted hallway behind Burns.

Well, Burns told himself, there was one sure way to find

out who was calling. He went back into the office and picked up the phone.

"Carl Burns," he said.

"Burns. I'm glad I caught you in your office. I was somehow under the impression that the faculty didn't hang around the campus on Friday afternoon."

It was Franklin Miller, HGC's president. Burns had no idea what he could want.

"Some of us dedicated professionals do," Burns said, glad that he'd stayed around for once.

"Excellent," Miller said. "Excellent."

Burns didn't know how to respond to that, so he just waited.

"As I was saying," Miller went on, "I'm glad I caught you in your office. There's something I wanted to discuss with you."

Burns's day, which he had begun in such a good mood, was going downhill rapidly. It was never good news when the president wanted to have a talk with you, especially late on a Friday afternoon.

"Do you want me to come to your office?" Burns asked.

"No. No, I don't think so. I think I'll come over there."

That would be a first. As far as Burns knew, no HGC president had ever climbed up to the third floor of Main. Miller must have something really serious on his mind.

"Do you know where my office is?" Burns asked, just to be sure Miller knew what he was getting into.

"I think I can find it. It's on the third floor of Main, isn't it?"

Burns said that it was.

"Excellent. I can find it, then. I suppose that there's hardly anyone else around?"

It was a question, so Burns said, "Just Eric Holt. Unless he's gone home."

"Why don't you check on that?"

Burns said that he would.

"Excellent," Miller said. "I'll be there in fifteen minutes."

Burns told him that he'd be waiting.

* * *

Not quite fifteen minutes had passed when Miller appeared at Burns's door. He must have been in better shape than Burns would have guessed; he was panting only slightly.

"Those stairs are quite steep, aren't they?" he said. He was wearing a dark blue suit and a subdued maroon tie.

"They are," Burns agreed. "You can see why Dean Partridge is talking about an elevator."

The thought of an elevator, and its cost, made Miller frown. Burns asked him to come in and sit down.

"I hate to intrude on your Friday," Miller said as he settled himself into the chair. "Did you look in on Eric Holt, by the way?"

Burns had, but Holt had already left.

Miller thought that was excellent. "Ordinarily I wouldn't have asked about that. It's just that I needed to speak to you privately." He glanced around. "So there's no one else around, then?"

"No. Eric's always the last to leave."

"Excellent." Miller relaxed fractionally. "There are several things I want to go over with you."

"All right," Burns said, wondering what they could be and knowing with grim certainty that they weren't going to make him happy.

"One is this 'looksism' business. I suppose you've heard about it."

Burns admitted that he had.

"Of course. Everyone on campus has. And a few people in town, as well. That young woman who brought the accusation. Bunni. She's your student secretary, isn't she?"

"Yes. And a very good one."

"I'm sure she is. But this looksism business, Burns, isn't good at all. It's going to cause trouble, and it's going to be a black eye for the college if it's not handled correctly. You can see that, can't you?"

Burns could see it, all right. He'd already thought about it when talking to George. "But there's not really much we can do about that, is there?"

Miller shook his head. "I'm afraid not. I just don't know what got into Dean Partridge when she sent all those memos. I tried to explain to her that we're a small school, a conservative school, maybe even an old-fashioned school."

No maybe to it, Burns thought. HGC was definitely all of those things.

"But she had all these new ideas," Miller continued. "And I thought that was good, in its own way. I thought that maybe we had become complacent, set in our ways, afraid of change. I thought it might be to the school's benefit to have someone new coming in, someone with new ideas and fresh approaches to the old problems."

It was true that the school and most of the people who worked there didn't like the idea of change, Burns thought. But why change when you were doing a good job? Well, Eric Holt could no doubt tell anyone why, but Burns wasn't sure that he would agree.

"Dr. Holt has certainly brought some new ideas into my department," he said.

"I've heard a little about that. Does he really talk about comic books?"

"Sometimes," Burns said.

Miller shook his head. "I'm not sure I understand everything that's going on in education these days, Burns."

"I'm not sure that I do, either, if that's any comfort."

"It's good to know I'm not alone," Miller said, not sounding convinced. "But what I wanted to ask was whether there was anything you could do to help out in this looksism business."

"I'm not sure there is. I did agree to speak for George Kaspar at the hearing."

"Excellent. Excellent. I can't think of anyone I'd rather have on my side. I'm sure you'll represent him well and at the same time do whatever is best for HGC."

"I'll try," Burns said. He lacked Miller's confidence. "It's not easy to predict how something like that might turn out."

"I'm not as worried about that as I was, now that I know

you're on the case. That's very good news." Miller rubbed his hands together. "Now. There's one other thing that's been worrying me."

Here it comes, Burns thought. *I've been buttered up sufficiently for him to get to the real heart of the matter.*

"It's about Tom Henderson," Miller said.

"Oh," Burns said.

"Yes. A bad business, and it's not going to look good for Hartley Gorman College. Not good at all, what with Dean Elmore's death and then Street getting killed when we invited him here for the seminar. But you were very helpful in those unfortunate events, Burns. Very helpful."

"I didn't really do anything," Burns protested. Now he knew where the conversation was leading.

"You certainly did do something. Of course I wasn't here for the Elmore business, thank goodness, but I know what you did about the Street matter. If it hadn't been for you, the police would most likely have botched it."

That wasn't strictly true, but Miller had made up his mind, and Burns wasn't going to bother trying to convince him otherwise.

"And so," Miller said, "I'd like to think that you were working with Chief Napier on this case as well. Then I'd know that matters were well in hand."

"I saw Bo—Chief Napier on campus the other day," Burns said. "We talked, and I've been trying to do what I can, but I wouldn't say that I've accomplished much."

"Nonsense. I'm sure you've accomplished a great deal. Yes, indeed. That's the best news I've heard all day. I don't have to tell you, Burns, that I'm worried about this. It affects us all when someone dies under mysterious circumstances, as Tom did. But I'm sure you'll have everything solved before the weekend's over."

Burns felt a momentary stab of panic. "That might be rushing things a little."

Miller reached out and tapped Burns on the knee. "Modesty. That's a quality that I've always admired in men of accomplishment, Burns. You're much better at this sort of thing than you want to admit." He stood up. "Remember, I'm counting on you. And don't hesitate to call on me if I can do anything at all to assist you."

"I'll do that," Burns said.

Miller walked to the door. "And, Burns?"

"Yes?"

"It's good to see you here so late on a Friday. Most of the faculty don't take their responsibilities as seriously as you do."

"I wouldn't say that, sir," Burns told him.

"Modesty," Miller said, and laughed. He gave Burns a salute and walked away.

Burns started to get up and leave, but he didn't. The conversation with Miller had left him too depressed. So he sank back in his chair and brooded.

At seven-thirty that evening, Burns's doorbell rang. He wondered who it could be. He didn't often have callers at home.

He reluctantly put down the copy of *You'll Die Next!*, the Harry Whittington classic that he was reading, then went to the door and opened it. Boss Napier stood on the mat outside. If George Kaspar had looked unhappy, Napier looked furious.

"Hello, Burns," he said. "It's good to see that you're having a nice quiet evening at home."

"I'm only here because I couldn't get a date," Burns said. He had spoken to Elaine on Thursday evening about going out on Friday, but she had told him she would be busy. Probably with Napier, Burns had surmised, though she hadn't said that. Anyway, if Napier had gone out with her, things clearly hadn't turned out very well.

"You going to make me stand out here all night?" Napier asked.

Burns stepped back from the door, holding it open. "Not at all. Come on in."

Napier walked into the house. He didn't wait for an

invitation to sit down. He dropped into the first chair he came to.

"Can I get you a Pepsi?" Burns asked, trying to be a good host.

Napier wasn't impressed. "Don't try to cozy up to me, Burns. I know what's going on."

"Well, I don't," Burns said, though he was afraid that he probably did. "Why don't you tell me."

Napier settled back in his chair. "All right. I will. But first why don't you define 'looksism' for me."

"So that's it."

"That's it, all right, and don't tell me you didn't know something about it." Napier stood up. "If I had my bullwhip here, Burns—"

So the bullwhip rumor was true. Or maybe it wasn't. Maybe it was just something Napier liked to talk about to scare people. Well, he wasn't going to scare Burns.

"You can't blame me for this," Burns said. "I didn't have a thing to do with it. In fact, I don't even know what you're talking about."

Napier wasn't going to be put off that easily. "You teach at that school, don't you? And that's where all this Looney Tunes business started, isn't it? You can't weasel out of it, Burns. You know exactly what I'm talking about."

That wasn't strictly true, but Burns didn't think it would do any good to split hairs. "I'm not trying to weasel out of anything. But none of this politically correct stuff was my idea."

Napier sat back down. "So that's it. Political correctness. I should've known."

"Why?" Burns asked, surprised.

Napier gave him a hard look. "You think I don't know what's going on in the world, don't you, Burns? You think I'm a real dummy, and all I do is watch 'Hawaii Five-0' reruns in my spare time, isn't that right?"

Burns was well aware of Napier's fondness for Steve McGarrett and the men of the Hawaii State Police. "I know you like to paint model soldiers, too."

"Yeah. Right. That and watch TV. But that's not all, Burns. I even read newspapers and magazines occasionally. So I know a little about political correctness and how it's the big thing on college campuses these days."

Burns was curious. "Well, what do you think of it?"

"I think it's cultural Nazism, that's what I think. It's not just in the schools, either, Burns. It's all around us. I read that in some city in Canada you can't even call a manhole cover a manhole cover anymore, not if you work for the city. You have to call it a maintenance access cover. What would an English teacher think about that?"

Burns thought it was about the same thing as calling a toothbrush a home plaque-removal implement, though the purpose was slightly different. Not all that different if you thought about it, however.

"I think it's stupid," Napier said. "I don't mind calling a fireman a fire fighter, and I don't see anything wrong with talking about mail carriers instead of mailmen. But *maintenance access covers*? It's just stupid, if you ask me. That's off the subject, though, and it's not what I came here to talk about."

Too bad, Burns thought. If Napier had gotten sidetracked, it might have been easier all around. In fact, the idea was so appealing that Burns tried again to steer Napier away from the subject of looksism.

"I'm sure you didn't come here to talk about anything that trivial," he said. "You probably came to talk about Tom Henderson's murder."

Napier's jaw tightened. "The murder. No, Burns, that's not really why I came here. But you're right. Maybe this other stuff is just trivial, considering that someone's been killed. So let's talk about that. Let's talk about the murder."

Burns started to relax.

But not for long. Napier glared at him. "And then we'll talk about Elaine Tanner and looksism and what a low-life backstabber you are."

"All right," Burns said weakly.

"Yeah," Napier said. "But now let's talk about the murder. You go first, Burns."

So Burns went first, thinking about the story of Scheherazade, although he was afraid that he couldn't hold out for a thousand and one nights, as appealing as the idea was to him. Napier wouldn't let him get away with it.

His only hope was that Napier would get so caught up in the murder case that he wouldn't remember his real purpose in visiting. Somehow, Burns didn't think that would happen, but it was worth a try.

14

IN FACT, BURNS didn't last anywhere near a thousand and one nights. He didn't last even fifteen minutes, for the simple reason that he didn't have that much to say. He didn't want to make any accusations about Melling or Holt because he didn't really know anything for sure. Of course he knew that Melling had lied at first about being in Henderson's office, and he was convinced that Melling hadn't told the whole truth even yet, but that didn't make the man a killer.

Holt was obviously concealing something as well, but what he was concealing might not be murder. Then again, it might be, but Burns wasn't sure of that.

And Burns hadn't even talked to Kristi Albert yet. He was planning to do that on Saturday if he could find her after Henderson's funeral.

So all he could do was tell Napier that he was "looking into things" and mention that Henderson had something of a reputation as a womanizer or at least as someone who was not above a little sexual harassment now and then.

"But not to hear his wife tell it," Burns went on. "Her version of the story is that Henderson was irresistible to women. They were the ones who came on to him instead of the other way around."

"You've been talking to your buddies, haven't you?" Napier said.

"Not since early this morning. Why?"

"I talked to their wives about Henderson. Mrs. Henderson

told me that both of them were after her husband and that their husbands might have done him in."

"You didn't believe that, did you?"

"I never believe anybody in a murder case, Burns."

Burns tried to look offended. "Does that include me?"

"Especially you. Anyway, those two women told me that things were just about the opposite of what Mrs. Henderson had said. *Some*body's lying, right?"

"Right," Burns agreed. "Samantha Henderson."

"I wouldn't be so sure about that, Burns. You never can tell who some women might be attracted to."

"That's probably a sexist remark," Burns told him.

"Maybe. But if it is, I don't care. Let's just call it an observation based on my experience. Not everyone is attracted to physical appearances."

Burns studied Napier's face to see if there was a double meaning in the police chief's words, but it was like looking at a weathered stone. Napier revealed nothing.

"Did Mrs. Henderson mention anyone else?" he asked.

"Yeah. Somebody named Spelling. Used to be a big-time football player, but now he works at the college. I haven't talked to him or his wife yet."

"Melling," Burns said. "He's a recruiter."

"That's him. Mrs. Henderson says his wife used to be all over her husband."

"She's wrong," Burns said.

"That's what you say. How do you know? Have you talked to her?"

"As a matter of fact, I have. Her story is a lot different."

"I'll get around to her, and her husband, too. But that won't let your pals off the hook. Their wives, either."

"Well," Burns said, "if you think Joynell Tomlin or Rae Fox would be interested in Tom Henderson, you're not as experienced a cop as I think you are."

The mild jibe didn't bother Napier in the least. "Maybe I'm not. Anything else, Burns?"

"There is one thing. I'd like you to run a check on

someone through your computer setup. You can do that, can't you?"

"Run somebody through the computer? Sure. I can do that. But didn't you mean to ask me if I *will* do it?"

Now Napier was lecturing him on the use of "can" and "will." Would wonders never cease? Maybe there was a frustrated English teacher lurking under the tough-cop exterior.

"Yes," Burns said. "That's what I meant to ask you. *Will* you do that for me?"

"Okay. Now which of your buddies do you want to know about?"

Burns was surprised it had been so easy. "It's not one of my buddies. It's not even someone I know."

Napier was puzzled. "What does this have to do with Henderson's murder, then?"

"I'm not really sure," Burns admitted.

"That's great, Burns. Just great. Now let me be sure I've got this straight. You haven't found out anything about anybody, and you're sure that I'm wrong if I think your buddies might be involved, not to mention this Melling, but you want me to run a name through the National Crime Information Center just out of idle curiosity."

"That covers it pretty well," Burns said.

"Okay. What's the name?"

Napier had surprised Burns again. "You're going to give in just like that?"

"Why not? You'll tell me the rest of it when you get around to it. But don't blame me if whatever you're sitting on gets you in big trouble."

"I won't." It was an easy promise to make. Burns didn't see how anything he knew could cause him a problem.

"So what's the name?" Napier asked.

"Mitchum," Burns said. "Henry Mitchum."

"That's it?"

"Also known as Hank."

"And after I run the name through? Then what?"

"You tell me what you find out."

"Fine." Napier took out a pocket-sized spiral notebook and wrote something in it with a Bic pen. Then he shut the notebook and looked at Burns. "And that's it?"

"That's it."

"You're sure there's nothing else? You don't want me to fix a few speeding tickets for you while I'm at it?"

Burns wasn't going to be baited. "No. But thanks for asking."

"Don't mention it," Napier said. He had a thoughtful look. "Funny thing. That name seems familiar to me for some reason."

"Do you watch 'America's Most Wanted'?" Burns asked, wondering whether Mal Tomlin could have been right.

"Is that what this is? You've seen some wanted felon on TV and you want me to check him out?"

"No," Burns said. "It was just something that popped into my head. Forget it."

Napier opened his notebook and stared at what he'd written. "I don't know. It's like I've heard the name before, but I can't remember where. You ever get that feeling, Burns?"

Burns was having it now, sort of. He was thinking that there was something that he had heard in the last couple of days that he'd interpreted incorrectly, but he couldn't think what it might be. However, he thought that if he could only figure it out, he'd have a completely different outlook on Tom Henderson's murder.

"I've had the feeling," he said. "But it doesn't make much difference, does it? Not unless we can tie it to Tom Henderson. Why don't you tell me what you've found out?"

Napier told him, but it didn't add anything to what Burns already knew. Actually, Napier hadn't found out anything of any significance. So far, his chief suspects were Tomlin and Fox, which was patently ridiculous. Napier and his men clearly weren't as good at investigation as Burns was.

Or maybe Burns just happened to be in a better position to hear things.

"It's not going so well, is it?" Burns said.

"Nope," Napier said. "It's not. Unless your buddies happen to be guilty. Then I'd say it was going pretty well, wouldn't you?"

"Not for them."

"Right. I bet they're counting on you to clear them, Burns. Think you can do it?"

"Counting on me? Have you arrested them?"

"Not yet. Not enough evidence for that. But we're looking."

"You won't find anything."

"You might be surprised. But like I said, they're probably counting on you to keep them in the clear. You're not doing so hot, though, are you?"

"We'll see," Burns said.

"Yeah, I guess we will. And now let's have a little talk about looksism."

"Let me get something to drink first," Burns said, hoping to postpone the discussion a little longer. "You're sure you don't want a Pepsi?"

Napier gave in. "Okay, bring me one. But it's not going to get you off the hook."

Burns hadn't thought that it would.

When Napier finally left it was after eleven o'clock. As it turned out to his credit, he didn't really blame Burns for Elaine's accusations. And besides, as Napier himself admitted, "She's probably right. I wouldn't have been attracted to her if she weren't a dynamite looker. Anyway, she didn't really mean it when she told me not to come around anymore. I could tell her heart wasn't in it."

"What's bothering you, then?" Burns wanted to know.

"What's bothering me is that she thinks you like her because she's smart, not because she looks great."

"She's right," Burns said.

He tried not to feel smug, and didn't mention that what he *really* liked about Elaine was that she was smart and looked great at the same time. He wondered, however, why

Elaine was suddenly giving him so much credit, while at the same time revising her opinion of Napier. Maybe it was because he had discussed the case with her and sought her opinion. Napier was likely to discuss things, true, but not nearly as likely as Burns to ask for advice.

"Baloney," Napier said. "I know you better than you think I do, Burns. You might read poetry and all that, but you've got eyes. You know what Elaine looks like, and that's for sure."

Burns didn't say anything.

"That's all right," Napier told him. "She'll catch on to you sooner or later. And then I'll move in again. Or maybe she'll just want to talk cop talk with somebody. She really likes that stuff, you know."

Burns knew. And he suspected that Napier was right about moving in again. But he was going to enjoy his advantage while he could.

"There's just one more thing," Napier said as he was leaving. "I know you've found out more than you're telling me, and that's all right. But you might think about what's happened to you in the past when you got in over your head. I might not be there to save you this time."

"I'll keep that in mind," Burns said.

After Napier was gone, Burns found that he wasn't ready for bed, but he couldn't get back to his reading. Something was bothering him, and he went back over every conversation he'd had recently, letting each play back in his mind word for word, or as near word for word as he could come. He was pretty sure that he was nowhere near. Maybe he should buy himself a little notebook like Napier's and write things down.

Recalling the conversations was good mental exercise, but it didn't provide Burns with any new clues. He told himself that maybe things would become clear while he slept. He would wake up on Saturday with a head full of clues and the name of the killer on the tip of his tongue.

Or then again, maybe he wouldn't.

*   *   *

He didn't. He woke up thinking how much he hated to give up his Saturday morning for something like a funeral. Then he told himself that he was even more selfish than he'd thought and rolled out of bed, trying not to resent the fact that he'd have to wear a suit and tie.

The funeral was at ten o'clock, which meant that he wouldn't have to wear the suit all day, just most of the morning. There was that to be thankful for. But before he changed, he intended to look up Kristi Albert. If she lived in the women's dorm, she would be easy to find.

He got up, dressed, and read the paper while eating a bowl of Frosted Mini Wheats. He wasn't reading the Pecan City paper, which didn't publish on Saturdays. It was the Dallas *Morning News*. Burns subscribed because he liked the comic strips, which he considered more relevant to real life than most of what the paper published. He wouldn't have been surprised if Eric Holt agreed with him on that.

After finishing his breakfast and the comics, Burns read some more from *You'll Die Next!* Then it was time to leave for the funeral.

He drove to the church in his Plymouth and didn't have any trouble finding a place to park. There wasn't going to be a huge crowd.

Henderson's casket was down in front of the altar, and it was closed, for which Burns was grateful. He didn't want to have to say any last good-byes. He looked over the pews to see who was there. Walt and Dawn Melling were sitting near the back. The Tomlins and the Foxes were sitting together, and Burns was on his way to join them until he saw Elaine Tanner. She moved over and he slid in beside her.

He was going to whisper "Good morning," but he wasn't sure that would be appropriate. They were at a funeral, after all. So he just smiled, sadly.

Elaine nodded, and then her eyes went past him to someone else. Burns looked to the side and there was Boss Napier standing in the aisle.

Elaine didn't say anything, but she slid over some more,

making room. Burns didn't see anything to do but the same. Napier sat beside him.

Burns thought of asking him what he was doing there, but it wasn't necessary. Napier told him.

"You never know what'll happen at a funeral," Napier whispered. "Sometimes you can learn a lot from people's reactions."

Burns nodded as if he had known this all along. Napier didn't have anything else to say.

The crowd trickled in slowly, most of them from the college. Dean Partridge came in, along with Eric Holt, though they didn't sit together. All the members of Burns's department were there as well. Henderson didn't seem to have made too many friends outside the school, though there were ten or twelve people that Burns didn't recognize. He wondered if any of them had a motive to kill Henderson. By the time the service was to begin, there were more people there than Burns had really expected.

The pipe organ played softly in the background, mostly slow, lugubrious hymns that Burns hoped no one would play at his own funeral. Some of the songs had either too many sharps or too many flats for the organist to handle, and when she hit the wrong key several people would wince slightly.

After what seemed like a very long time, Samantha Henderson and her family entered. Her mother was beside her. There was a man who looked a little like Tom—this was undoubtedly his father—along with several cousins and some older people who must have been aunts and uncles.

Samantha's eyes were glittery and damp as she looked at the casket, but when she looked out at the crowd and saw the Foxes and Tomlins, the eyes changed and took on an almost feral light. Burns hoped that she didn't do anything unseemly.

She didn't. She was seated by her mother, and the minister began talking, saying the soothing things that ministers are supposed to say but that somehow didn't seem very comforting to Burns. He hoped the family found them more reassuring than he did.

The congregation sang a hymn, "How Great Thou Art," and the minister launched into his praise of Tom Henderson, most of which Burns thought was pretty inflated, considering what he knew of Henderson's character. Then there was a brief sermon, though not brief enough for Burns.

After the sermon and another song, this one sung by one of HGC's music instructors, the funeral was over and the casket was being rolled down the aisle, with the family walking along behind. Burns allowed himself to relax. It hadn't been as bad as it might have been.

Samantha Henderson was weeping openly now, leaning on her mother. Fortunately the organ served to drown out the sounds of her sobbing.

When Samantha reached the row where the Tomlins and Foxes were sitting, she suddenly stopped and straightened up. Her mother looked surprised and put a hand on Samantha's elbow as if to urge her along.

Burns didn't like the looks of this. He was afraid that Samantha might yet make a scene. Burns didn't like scenes.

Samantha's mother was whispering something to her daughter, but Samantha wasn't listening. Her sobbing had stopped.

"What's the matter?" Elaine asked in a low voice. Whispers were beginning to break out all over the church.

Burns didn't answer her. He was about to say something to Boss Napier, but he saw that the police chief was watching with a great deal of interest and had no intention of intervening.

Then Samantha Henderson yelled something that sounded to Burns suspiciously like "Man-stealing bitches!" and made a dive toward Joynell Tomlin.

▽

15

THINGS HAPPENED FAST after that. Joynell and Samantha went down into the space between the pews and disappeared from Burns's sight, though he, like everyone else in the building, was standing on tiptoe trying to see what was going on.

There were several screeches and what sounded to Burns like a couple of dull thuds, but he couldn't tell what was happening. There were so many people crowded around the pew by then that there was no hope of seeing anything.

The minister was trying to fight his way through the crowd, but he wasn't having much success. No one wanted to give up his (or, Burns reminded himself, her) place for fear of missing something. Finally the minister resorted to trying to get everyone's attention by shouting.

"This is a church! This is a house of God!" he said. But that didn't do any good either. No one was paying him the least attention.

Meanwhile, the organist, apparently oblivious to what was going on, kept playing the same slow, mournful hymns. She was, however, playing them louder. Burns knew that, because he could hear them clearly over the talking and shouting that would ordinarily have drowned them out.

Napier just stood there, watching like everyone else.

The organist hit a sour note on "Softly and Tenderly" just as Joynell Tomlin, or maybe it was Samantha Henderson, screamed. There was another thud from the direction of the pew.

Burns, who was embarrassed by the whole thing, poked Napier in the back. "Why don't you do something?"

"I told you," Napier said, seeming quite cheerful. "You never can tell what you might learn at a funeral."

The organist reached the chorus, and the words in Burns's mind were punctuated by the shrieks of Joynell and her adversary.

"Earnestly, tenderly, Jesus is calling—"

"Eeeeeeeeeeee!"

"—calling, O sinner—"

"Aaarrrrrrrrrggggghhh!"

"—Come home!"

Burns was about to give another try at poking Napier into action, but then he saw Joynell Tomlin rise up, her beehive a disordered mess. He suspected that at least one of the screams had come when Samantha yanked a handful of it. Joynell's lipstick was smeared across her cheek. Or maybe it was Samantha's lipstick.

Joynell had her hands on Samantha's shoulders, and she was propelling the grieving widow back into the aisle. The crowd suddenly fell silent, and those around the pew moved away to make room.

". . . and try to act dignified!" Joynell said as she shoved Samantha into the waiting arms of her family.

Samantha looked as if she wanted to make another dive at Joynell, but her mother and her father-in-law restrained her. Joynell glowered at her and straightened her dress. Mal stood beside his wife, looking mortified. Burns didn't blame him, although Joynell didn't look upset at all. A little disheveled, maybe, but not upset.

The pallbearers had successfully gotten the casket out of the church during the interruption, but the aisle was packed with curious onlookers. They returned to their seats, and Samantha and her family walked slowly on out of the church. Instead of the usual respectful silence, there was the buzz of many whispered conversations. Burns thought he could guess the topic of every one of them.

"Still think your buddies didn't have anything to do with the murder?" Napier asked.

Burns just shook his head.

Samantha and her family didn't linger outside the church for the traditional words of comfort from friends. They piled into the waiting limousine for the ride to the cemetery and sat there behind the closed doors and rolled-up windows. Burns suspected that the family was holding Samantha under house arrest to keep her from creating any more incidents.

Napier pulled Burns aside as they left the building and jerked his head toward a towering pecan tree near the street. Burns asked Elaine to wait for him and walked with Napier to the tree, away from the crowd, most of whom were still talking about what had happened inside.

"I got a question for you, Burns," Napier said.

"What? And why didn't you put a stop to that fight?"

"That wasn't any of my business. Just shows that Mrs. Henderson really believes those women are to blame."

"They aren't."

"So you say. But I want to ask you about something else. That name you gave me."

A breeze moved the leaves of the pecan tree, rustling them together. A car hummed by in the street. Burns watched it move on down the block.

"Did you check on the name?" he asked.

"Yeah. And now I know why I remembered it. Maybe you were right. Maybe I saw it on 'America's Most Wanted.' I'm sure there was a show on the guy, but it could have been 'Unsolved Mysteries'."

Burns couldn't believe it. "You're kidding."

"Nope. Now what I want to know is why you wanted me to check on that name."

"I was just curious. I ran across it somewhere."

"Don't try to mess with me, Burns."

"I'm not." Curiosity filled Burns. "Tell me what you found out."

Napier brought out his little notebook, scanned a page, and said, "Mitchum is one of those radicals from the seventies who got himself in a heap of trouble and then just disappeared. Nobody's seen or heard from him in twenty years."

Or maybe he has been heard from, Burns thought. *Maybe he's been around all along, under another name.*

"I don't remember seeing the story," he said. "What kind of trouble are we talking about?"

"According to him, he didn't do anything."

"Then why would he be on one of those crime shows?"

"Because, according to the FBI, he *did* do something. He was part of a bank robbery in California. He was the driver of the getaway car."

Good lord, Burns thought.

Napier leaned his back against the tree and put a foot up on the trunk. "His story was that he was just a victim. Four guys kidnapped him at gunpoint, forced him to drive to the bank, and one of them held a pistol on him while the other three went in and committed the robbery."

"Who were the guys?" Burns asked.

"Part of some bunch that called themselves FTP, Free the People. They were going to use the money from the bank to overthrow the government, or whatever. But something went wrong. Mitchum and the guy with the gun took off in his car, but they wound up wrapped halfway around a light pole after a high-speed chase. The guy with the gun was killed, but Mitchum survived."

Burns wasn't sure he wanted to know the answer to his next question. "What about the guys in the bank?"

"All three of them were killed. One of the tellers tripped a silent alarm, and they were trapped in the bank. There was a shoot-out with the police . . . a guard got shot and died. There's always been a little suspicion that no one meant to kill him and that he just got caught in the cross fire, but the robbers took the blame."

"How did Mitchum get away from the police if he was hurt in the wreck?"

"He was in the hospital, under guard. He'd given his story to the police, but nobody believed him, and he probably knew it. He was a student, and apparently pretty well known as a campus agitator. He'd been associated with plenty of radical groups. FTP wasn't one of them, but the fact that he was in the car with them was suspicious to everyone. It didn't look good for him, so he got his hands on somebody's scrub suit and slipped out. That's the last time anyone ever saw him."

Napier folded his notebook closed and stuck it into a pocket. Burns looked back at the thinning funeral crowd. The hearse was pulling away from the curb for the drive to the cemetery. A number of cars followed it.

Elaine stood near the church entrance with the Tomlins and the Foxes. Joynell was talking and waving her hands. Considering what had just happened inside, Mal and Joynell probably didn't feel much like going to the burial site.

"So now I guess you better explain why you wanted to know about that guy," Napier said. "That's a pretty funny name just to pick out of a hat."

"It's just a name I ran across," Burns said, thinking that he was telling the absolute truth.

"I believe that," Napier told him. "Like I believe the government is going to repeal the income tax. So explain how you happened to run across it just now. And why did you want me to run it through the computer? I remember seeing an old San Diego State yearbook in Henderson's office, and that's where this Mitchum went to school. Is there some connection between the two of them?"

"I don't know," Burns said, and that was also the truth, even if it didn't tell the whole story.

Napier looked over to where Elaine was still talking to Joynell Tomlin. "I'm already chapped at you, Burns, or did you not notice that Elaine didn't even speak to me today?"

Burns had noticed, but he hadn't wanted to say anything. No use in rubbing it in.

"So that's one mark against you," Napier said. "Now it begins to look a whole lot like you're holding out on me. If you've got something on this Mitchum, I want to know about it now."

Burns told the truth once again. "I don't have anything. Let's just say it's something I'm looking into."

"You're going to get in trouble again, Burns," Napier said, shaking his head. "I know it."

"I'll let you know as soon as I find out anything for sure. Trust me."

"Ha ha," Napier said. But he wasn't laughing. He wasn't even smiling.

By the time Burns got back to Elaine, Mal and Earl were nowhere to be seen, and Joynell had finished telling her story. Burns was sorry he had missed it. Joynell had a way of improving things in the telling, and he was sure that by now the tale of Samantha's unprovoked attack had reached epic proportions. He was about to ask her to repeat it when Mal appeared from around the side of the church, waving his hand wildly in a signal for Burns to join him.

Burns excused himself and walked over to where Tomlin was standing beside Earl Fox in the shade of the building.

"We caught 'em!" Tomlin said, punching his right fist into his left palm.

Fox was as excited as his friend. "That's right. Red-handed!"

"Good," Burns said. "Who did you catch?"

He was glad Napier wasn't listening. The police chief would probably have told him that "whom" was the correct word.

"Partridge and Holt," Fox said. "Who else?"

"If you caught them, where are they?"

"We didn't catch 'em in a trap," Tomlin said. "We caught 'em talking together."

"Oh," Burns said. "That sounds serious. Is there a law against it?"

Tomlin was disgusted. "Look, we're just trying to help. If you want those two to get away with murder, just say so."

Burns was tempted to say "So" and let it go at that, but Tomlin's hunch about "America's Most Wanted" hadn't been that far off the mark.

"All right," he said. "Tell me about it."

"Okay," Tomlin said. "I'd heard enough about Joynell and that crazy Henderson woman, and I was tired of the way people were looking at us, so Earl and I decided to sneak off behind the church for a cigarette."

No surprise in that, Burns thought, though Earl usually wouldn't smoke right out in the open.

"There's a big bush back there," Tomlin said. "You've seen it."

He was right. A huge ligustrum of some kind grew beside the back steps; Burns had seen it many times.

"There's some space between that bush and the wall," Tomlin went on. "We stepped back in there and lit up. You can hardly even see the sidewalk."

"And they came walking right up to us," Fox said. "We could practically reach out and touch them."

Tomlin laughed. "Fox was so scared the dean would catch him smoking that he nearly fainted. He didn't know whether to eat his cigarette or just die right there."

"What did you do?" Burns asked.

The question was directed to Fox, but it was Tomlin who answered. "He threw it down and stepped on it. But very quietly. They didn't hear a thing. And that's when they started talking."

"About Henderson's murder?"

"No," Tomlin said. "But it was almost as good. Partridge told Holt to come to her house tonight, and they'd 'talk things over.' "

Burns didn't think that was particularly incriminating. He suspected that they were planning to discuss the impending appearance of George (The Ghost) Kaspar before the student court.

"What's wrong with talking things over?" he asked.

Tomlin looked at Burns as he might look at a student who

had just asked a really stupid question. "Don't you get it?
She was probably talking about Henderson. They know
you're getting close and they're scared."

"I think you're reading a lot into a simple conversation.
Boss Napier seems to think that you and Fox are much more
likely suspects than Holt and the dean."

"That's another thing," Tomlin said. "That cop asked
Joynell all kinds of questions about what was going on
between her and Henderson, and he even had the nerve to
imply that I might have wanted Henderson out of the way
because I was jealous of him. Did you ever hear anything so
ridiculous?"

"Yes," Fox put in. "He implied the same thing about me."

"So that's even more reason why you have to pin it on
those two," Tomlin said. "You owe it to me and Earl."

"But what if they didn't do anything?"

"You've gotta be kidding! Didn't I just tell you we
heard them talking about it? You have to go over to her
house tonight and listen in on them. Get the facts and turn
them in."

"I can't go sneaking around the dean's house," Burns
protested. "That's crazy."

"Not if you catch a murderer," Tomlin pointed out. He
spread his hands. "If you're scared, I'll go with you."

"I'm not scared," Burns told him. "I just don't think it's
a good idea. We could get in big trouble."

Tomlin nudged him with an elbow. "Only if we get
caught," he said.

Harriet Kathryn Myers Hall was the HGC women's dormitory. Mrs. Myers, HGC class of 1949, had the good fortune
to marry well (which in 1949 would not have been considered a politically incorrect thing to do or say), and she had
been generous with the money that her oil-rich husband
lavished on her. Her most lasting contribution to HGC was
the dormitory, built ten years after her graduation, though
she had also given occasional gifts of money.

Elaine Tanner appreciated the monetary gifts more than the dorm, since Mrs. Myers had specified that the money be spent on books and periodical subscriptions for the library.

"It's an ugly building, isn't it?" Elaine said as she and Burns went inside.

Burns agreed with her, but he didn't think it was necessary to say so. The building probably wasn't any uglier than any other college dorm in the nation. Dorms weren't known for their architectural greatness.

The front room of the dorm was a large lobby-cum-sitting area, furnished with couches and chairs that had seen better days. One of the couches was covered with a hideous floral pattern that had probably been all the rage when the dormitory was built but that now looked very old-fashioned. The other couches didn't look much better.

This room was where the women of HGC could entertain their male friends, who were most definitely not allowed anywhere else in the building. HGC might have been becoming liberal in some of its attitudes, thanks to the influence of Dean Partridge, but it wasn't going to change into Berkeley overnight. Burns didn't doubt that the dean would eventually get around to challenging the old-fashioned rules of dorm life, but she couldn't do everything at once.

To one side of the sitting area was an office with a large window that overlooked the couches. There was always someone on duty in the office to be sure that there were no unauthorized visitors and that nothing untoward was happening between the couples on the couches.

There were several couples sitting around, talking and looking at textbooks. There wasn't even any hand-holding going on that Burns could see. Hartley Gorman College's students knew better than to indulge themselves in public displays of affection, though PDAs were no longer punishable by suspension as they had been in the distant past.

Burns went over to the office and asked if Kristi Albert was a dormitory resident.

"Yes, she is, Dr. Burns," the young woman behind the glass said. "She lives in 304."

"I'd like to talk to her," Burns said. "Would you call and see if she's in?"

She was, and Burns asked if she could come down. After a brief conversation on the phone, the young woman told Burns that Kristi would be down in five minutes.

"Want to sit down?" Burns asked Elaine. They went to one of the couches—not the one with the floral pattern, but a plain beige one that sagged badly.

"Do you really think I can be of some help, or did you just ask me to come to spite R.M.?" she asked when they were seated.

"I know you can help," Burns said, and then he saw someone come through the doorway that led to the stairs. It was the young woman he had seen running in tears from Henderson's office, and he knew that she must be Kristi Albert.

$$\triangledown$$

16

KRISTI ALBERT WAS short and stout, with her dark hair cut in bangs across her forehead. She wasn't big, Burns thought, but she was big enough to have pushed Henderson through his office window. He hadn't been very big either.

She frowned and did not look as if she were eager to talk to Burns, but she walked across the lobby to where he was sitting.

Burns stood up, which these days was probably not something a man was expected to do when a woman entered the room, but he couldn't help himself. He asked her name, and when she confirmed that she was Kristi Albert, he introduced her to Elaine.

Elaine, who had been coached by Burns on the way to the dorm, took over the conversation. Even talking to another woman, Kristi was clearly uncomfortable with the situation, and she shot covert glances at the other students in the room, all of whom were overly careful not to look in her direction.

"Is there somewhere we could go that's more private?" Elaine asked her.

"There's Mrs. Edgely's office," Kristi said. "She's not here today."

Dorinda Edgely was the dorm supervisor, and Burns was glad to hear that she wasn't around. She was a notorious snoop.

"Let's go see if we can use it," Elaine suggested.

Kristi assured them it would be all right. "She always leaves it open. I study in there sometimes."

Sure enough, the office was open. Even the light was on. Burns suspected that Dorinda was off shopping but had left the light on just in case any HGC administrator should happen to drop by. That way she could explain that she "just happened to step out for a minute."

Burns sat behind the polished wooden desk, while Elaine and Kristi sat on a couch that looked somewhat newer and more comfortable than those in the lobby. Elaine didn't drag things out. She let Kristi know immediately why they were there.

"I know you had some problems with Mr. Henderson," she said. "Why don't you tell me about them?"

Kristi cut her eyes toward Burns.

"He's not going to say anything," Elaine told her. "And he knows about Mr. Henderson."

"He saw me one day," Kristi said, still looking at Burns. "Coming out of Mr. Henderson's office."

"That's right," Elaine agreed. "He told me about that. Why were you there?"

Kristi looked back at Elaine. "I went to talk about a test. I thought I deserved a better grade than I got."

Burns thought that students these days had a lot more courage than those of his own generation, most of whom would never have dared to question their professors' right to give whatever grades they wanted to give.

"What did Mr. Henderson say about the grade?"

"I've talked about this to Dr. Fox," Kristi said. "But I don't want to say anything else. It doesn't seem right, not with Mr. Henderson being . . . passed away."

"I think you should tell me," Elaine said. "It might have something to do with the murder."

Elaine's saying the word like that seemed to shock Kristi. Her face reddened and she looked at the floor.

"There's something else, Kristi," Elaine said. "Someone saw you going to Mr. Henderson's office on the day he died."

Kristi's head snapped up. "Oh, no! I didn't. It wasn't me!"

Elaine looked at Burns.

"I'm afraid it was," he said, taking his cue and trying to make his voice appropriately hard. "You were there just before Mr. Henderson died."

Burns was amazed at his success. Kristi started crying. Elaine opened her purse, brought out a tissue, and handed it to Kristi, who took it and wiped her eyes.

"I'm sorry," she said, snuffling. "I shouldn't have lied. I did go to Mr. Henderson's office, but I didn't do anything to him. I was just talking to him about the test again."

She twisted the tissue in her hands, not looking at either Elaine or Burns, who was sure she was lying.

"Tell us your version of what happened the first time you went to see him," he said.

Kristi dabbed at her eyes with the wadded tissue. "He—he put his hand on me."

"Where?" Elaine asked.

Kristi didn't answer in words. Instead she moved her left hand to her breast.

"And is that when you ran away?" Burns asked.

"Yes. I told Dr. Fox about it later. He said he'd talk to the dean." Her eyes were dry now, and she looked resentful. "I didn't think he'd tell the whole school."

"He didn't," Burns said. "He just told me. This is murder we're talking about here, Kristi, not just sexual harassment. Dr. Fox thought it might be wiser for someone on the faculty to speak to you before the police found out."

"Oh! You aren't going to tell the police, are you?"

"No," Elaine said, giving Burns a look. "We aren't going to tell the police."

"Not if you tell us the truth," Burns said, not chastened by Elaine's glare. "Now, what did you say to Mr. Henderson on the day he was killed?"

Kristi looked at the wall, then at the floor, and finally back at Burns. "Nothing. I didn't even see him."

Burns was skeptical. "Are you sure about that?"

"You can tell us the truth, Kristi," Elaine said. "Nothing you say in here will leave this room."

Kristi didn't look as if she were sure of that. "That's what Dr. Fox said."

Burns stood up. "I think it's time to call Chief Napier," he said. "We're not getting anywhere."

"Wait!" Kristi said. "I'll tell you the whole thing."

"Fine," Burns said. "We're listening."

Clearly embarrassed, Kristi told her story. Knowing that Henderson had an evening class, she had gone to complain again about the grade, and she had gone alone in spite of what had happened previously. But she had a reason. She was planning to threaten Henderson.

"I was going to tell him that if he didn't do the right thing about my grade, I was going to tell his wife what he did to me."

Considering what Samantha Henderson seemed to think about her husband's attractiveness to women, Kristi would probably not have been believed. Burns thought it was more likely that Samantha would have accused Kristi of trying to seduce Tom.

"You were *going* to tell him," Burns said. "Did you?"

"No. Like I said, I never saw him. I couldn't do it. I started thinking about what he'd done, and how it made me feel, and I couldn't even go inside his office. I just turned around and went back downstairs. I didn't even know what had happened until a lot later."

"Did you see anyone else in his office or in the hallway?" Burns asked.

Kristi thought about it, then shook her head. "I don't remember. I don't think so."

Melling had seen her, however. There wasn't much question about that. She might have brushed by him in passing and not noticed, thanks to the stress she was feeling.

"I really do think he was being unfair about the grade," Kristi said. "My answers were a lot better than some others' that I could name. I just didn't sit in the right place. And maybe I don't have the right shape."

"I'm sure you had a good case," Burns said. "It's a little late to be worrying about that now, though."

"I guess it is," Kristi said. "But I still think I should have
a better grade."

"What did you think?" Elaine asked as she and Burns
walked the few blocks back to the church, where their cars
were parked. "Was she lying?"

"I don't know," Burns said. "She lied at first. Maybe she
was still lying at the end."

"How did we do as the good cop and the bad cop?"

"Not bad. Boss Napier would be proud of us."

Elaine frowned at the mention of Napier's name. "You
can see from what Kristi told us that sexual harassment has
its really dark side."

"I never doubted it. What does that have to do with
Napier?"

"Nothing. Exactly. But it's always the woman who suffers,
and he's not as enlightened as he should be. Maybe someone
needs to take him in hand and explain things to him."

Burns felt a momentary thrill of panic. He could imagine
what might happen if Napier got the chance to be alone with
Elaine while she tried to enlighten him. He didn't like the
idea of her "taking him in hand," either.

"I don't think so," he said. "Or then again, maybe it's a
good idea. I'll have a little talk with him."

Elaine smiled and took Burns's arm. "I like it when you're
jealous," she said.

That afternoon, Burns put some Creedence LPs on his turn-
table and tried to work out what he knew and what he
thought he knew while he listened to "Green River" and
"Born on the Bayou." What he knew wasn't much more
than he had known the last time he tried the exercise. He
still didn't know who was lying and who was telling the
truth. Walt Melling and Kristi Albert had, by their own
admission, both been in the vicinity of Henderson's office
on the day he was killed. Holt hadn't been seen there, but
he hadn't shown up for his class. His alibi was Dean

Partridge, which was suspicious in itself, as far as Burns was concerned.

And then there was the Henry Mitchum business. Burns was almost convinced that Holt and Mitchum were connected in some way. Maybe Holt *was* Mitchum. It wasn't really even a farfetched idea; lots of radicals from the seventies were still in hiding.

Burns had read about getting fingerprints by taking a person's water glass and giving it to the cops. He didn't know about the possibility of doing that, but there were any number of smooth-surfaced things he could take from Holt's office and turn over to Napier. It was worth thinking about.

And he wondered just how well fingerprints would show up on a bust of Sigmund Freud. All he had to do was locate it, and he could find out.

Burns turned that idea, and everything else, over and over in his mind, but the more he thought about things, the less he was sure he knew. And the more he developed the nagging feeling that he had overlooked something that he should have asked more about. Try as he would, he couldn't make it come clear.

Late in the afternoon, he gave up and read the rest of *You'll Die Next!* He had just set the book aside to make himself a ham sandwich when the telephone rang.

It was Mal Tomlin, who said he'd be by to pick Burns up at eight thirty.

"It'll be good and dark by then," Tomlin said. "That's the best time."

Burns didn't know what Tomlin was talking about. "Best time for what?"

"You know what. For catching them in the act."

Then Burns remembered. "I'm not going sneaking around anyone's house in the dark," he said. "You must be crazy."

Tomlin adopted a patient tone. "I'm not crazy. Just smart. Partridge and Holt are going to get together tonight, and they're going to talk about killing Henderson. If you'd heard them talking today, you'd know how worried they are. I'll be by at eight thirty. Wear something black. Do you have a black turtleneck?"

"Yes, but I'm not going to wear it," Burns said. "I'm not going anywhere with you on some half-baked spying expedition."

"Look," Tomlin said, "we have to do this. Your cop friend has scheduled another interview with Joynell for tomorrow. To clear up some 'discrepancies,' he says. He really thinks I had something to do with killing Henderson, and we have to prove he's wrong."

"But we can't prove anything by going over to Dean Partridge's house," Burns said.

There was a click on the other end of the line, but Burns continued to protest for another few seconds and before he realized that he was talking to dead air. He hung up the phone and made his sandwich. It didn't taste as good as he had thought it would.

He was wearing the black turtleneck, not to mention black jeans, and feeling like a fool when Mal Tomlin rang his doorbell at eight thirty.

Tomlin had on a similar outfit and his cheeks and forehead were covered with something dark and oily-looking.

"Smear some of this stuff on your face," Tomlin said. Still standing in the doorway, he handed Burns a tin can.

The outside of the can was slick, and Burns handed it back. "I'm not going to put that stuff on my face. What is it?"

"Some of that goop baseball players put under their eyes on bright days." Tomlin moved past Burns and into the house, sticking the can in Burns's hand. "You can put it on in here. We might want to wait a few more minutes before we go. They haven't rolled up the sidewalks yet. You got anything to eat?"

Burns looked into the can. "Where did you get this stuff?"

"Coach Thomas. You got any peanut butter and jelly?"

"Good grief," Burns said. "You told Coach Thomas about your idea for a commando raid?"

Tomlin grinned, his teeth looking very white in his blackened face. "I hadn't thought of it like that. A commando raid." He fell into a crouch and duckwalked across the den, pretending to be carrying an assault rifle. "Just like Arnold Schwarzenegger."

"You look more like a bad imitation of Chuck Berry," Burns said, laughing.

Tomlin straightened up. "You just don't appreciate style. Anyway, an army travels on its stomach. What about the peanut butter?"

"I have ham," Burns told him. "And mustard. Didn't Joynell feed you tonight?"

"Nope. She spent her time lecturing me about how stupid you and I were."

"She's right. If we do what I think we're going to do, we're even more stupid than she thinks."

"Yeah, well, we'll see how you feel after we get on 'America's Most Wanted' for cracking this case."

Burns thought about telling Tomlin about Henry Mitchum but decided against it. Tomlin was acting crazy enough already. The only good thing Burns could think of was that Tomlin wasn't armed. And if he knew that they might be encountering a man who took part, willingly or not, in an armed robbery in which a bank guard was killed, he'd insist on carrying an M16. If he could find one.

So Burns didn't mention Mitchum. Instead he asked, "What about Coach Thomas? What did you tell him to get this stuff?" He held up the can.

"I went by the gym after the funeral and told him that we were organizing a faculty baseball team. He gave me some old bats and balls, and I asked for a can of goop. If we handle this right, we can get some spikes, too. You want to play?"

"Are you serious?"

"Sure. I just wanted the black stuff, but the baseball team seems like a good idea. We could play the students in a charity game, maybe raise a little money for scholarships."

Napier didn't have a prayer of getting close to Elaine again, Burns thought. "Can I play second base?"

"Only if you put that stuff on your face."

Burns stuck a finger in the can. It came out black and greasy.

"Just rub it in," Tomlin said. "It won't hurt a bit."

Burns hesitated.

"Maybe we could get someone else to play second," Tomlin said. "Earl looks like an infielder. We'll see how he can handle a bat."

Burns smeared the greasy substance on his cheek. It wasn't so bad after all.

17

"WHAT REALLY WORRIES me is that damn goat," Tomlin said.

They were parked a long block from Dean Partridge's house, in a much more exclusive subdivision than Burns's. Here the homes were surrounded by towering pecan and oak trees and many of the houses sat on two or three lots to keep the neighbors at a proper distance.

The latter fact made things easier for a pair of prospective cat burglars, since the dean's home was set off from the others and the adjoining properties had wide yards of their own. Though the front yards were open to the street, the backyards were all surrounded by seven-foot wooden fences. Burns liked the protective aspect of the fences, but he wondered how in the world he and Tomlin were going to climb over one of them.

They were in Burns's car, parked in the alleyway that led down the block between two rows of houses, an alleyway that was generally traveled only by the local garbage trucks making regularly scheduled pickups. Burns had pulled his car in behind a big brown Dumpster, but it could still be seen from the street if anyone was looking.

Burns was worried about any number of things. He was almost sorry he didn't have a pen and paper so he could make a proper list. First, he was worried about climbing the high fence around the dean's backyard. Second, there was the fact that they were parked in an alley where any passing patrol car would probably spot them immediately. Third, there was the whole idea of sneaking around someone's house to see if two people were having a conference about a murder one of them had committed. And even if they were, how was anyone on the outside going to hear them? Burns was feeling more like a fool with every passing second, and then Tomlin had to go and mention the goat.

Burns had forgotten about the goat.

"I don't see why anyone would want a goat for a pet in the first place," Tomlin said.

"It's not a pet," Burns said, determined to be politically correct. "It's an animal companion."

"The hell it is."

Burns wasn't going to argue about it. "I don't want to talk about the goat. I want to know what kind of plan you have. If you have one."

Tomlin tried to look hurt, but he merely looked grotesque. The streetlight made the white flesh of his hands look green, and it made the greasepaint on his face look indescribable.

"Of course I have a plan," he said. "I've cased the joint."

"You *what*?"

"Cased the joint. I drove through the alley this afternoon after the funeral."

"Great. How many people do you think took your license number?"

"Give me a little credit, Burns. We were in Earl's car."

Burns moaned. He was doing a lot of that lately.

"Let's go," Tomlin said, ignoring him. "Don't slam the door when you get out."

Burns closed the door as quietly as he could, but it sounded to him as if someone had dropped one steel slab on top of another one. Tomlin evidently wasn't bothered, and by the time Burns had stopped cringing, Mal was halfway down the block.

Burns scuttled after him. He was holding a cheap plastic flashlight with weak batteries, the only one he had, but he was afraid to turn it on. The streetlight made things bright enough without it. Burns tried to stay in the shadows.

They stopped behind another Dumpster, practically in front of the gate in Dean Partridge's wooden fence. Tomlin was holding his finger to his lips, a completely unnecessary gesture, since Burns had no intention of saying a word.

After a second's pause to catch his breath, Tomlin slipped the latch on the gate and stepped through. Burns waited outside, hoping that Tomlin would forget about him, but Mal turned and motioned for Burns to follow. Reluctantly, he did.

"Checked it this afternoon," Tomlin whispered, closing the gate behind him.

Wouldn't want the goat to escape, Burns thought. He looked around the yard, but the animal companion was nowhere to be seen, though a certain unidentifiable but rank odor indicated that it was nearby, or recently had been. There was a low shed off to one side, well away from the fence; Burns assumed that this was the goat's shelter, though it could have been a storeroom for all he knew. If it was the former, he hoped that the goat was shut up inside for the night.

There were lights on in the dean's none-too-humble two-story abode, all of them on the lower floor. They illuminated yellow rectangles on the green grass, which was cropped close by the animal companion. Burns looked around again, but he still didn't see the goat.

Tomlin poked Burns in the shoulder and pointed toward a room that was obviously the kitchen. Eric Holt was sitting at a round table talking to Dean Partridge, who hadn't even bothered to draw the curtains.

And why bother? Burns thought. After all, no one could see inside from the alley, thanks to the fence. The dean had no reason to suspect that she was being watched by secret commando spies.

"We gotta get closer," Tomlin whispered. "They're talking about the murder."

Burns wondered how Tomlin could tell, but he didn't want to ask. He just followed his friend, who was duckwalking again, trying to stay in the shadow. Burns couldn't duckwalk very well; it was uncomfortable and demeaning, but it was better than slithering on his belly.

They got next to the window, staying on the right side, out of the light. Both of them had their heads against the wall, Burns high and Tomlin low, and they could hear the voices through the glass of the window.

Holt was doing most of the talking. Burns couldn't hear every word, but he could hear enough to get the gist. And the gist was enough to chill him, though the night was warm and the turtleneck was sweated through.

What he heard was something about the yearbook.

"It wasn't there. I used that passkey you gave me and looked. It's gone."

That was true. The yearbook was in Burns's office—at least it was if Holt was talking about the yearbook that had been on Henderson's desk. And what other yearbook was there to be concerned about?

That meant that Holt had almost certainly known about the picture of Mitchum, maybe had even discussed it with Henderson.

Dean Partridge said something about its not making any difference. "That picture won't mean a thing to the police. It's just one more photo in a book that's full of them."

Holt looked worried. Really worried. He said something that Burns didn't catch.

Partridge waved a hand in reply. "I'm telling you that they won't check every picture. They won't find out."

As far as Burns was concerned, that cinched it. He'd heard enough. He tapped Tomlin on the shoulder and hiked a thumb toward the fence.

Tomlin mouthed something that might have been "We just got here," but Burns paid him no mind. He was moving out.

And then he heard the prancing and pawing of four little hoofs.

The goat was standing on top of the shed, looking at him.

It was probably only Burns's imagination that the hard little horns glittered in the darkness.

"Son of a bitch," Tomlin said at Burns's back. "It's a guard goat."

The goat said, "B-a-a-a-a-a-a," and jumped off the shed. It charged across the yard, its head lowered.

"I take that back," Tomlin said, passing Burns at top speed. "It's an *attack* goat."

Tomlin, who was both faster and more agile than Burns, was opening the gate when the goat rammed Burns from behind.

The horns were just as hard as they'd looked. Burns rose up about a foot, flattened out, and sailed forward. His flashlight flew out of his hand and hit the fence. Burns then hit Tomlin right in the middle of the back.

Tomlin had the gate half open, but it slammed shut as he crashed into it. He and Burns landed in a writhing heap.

Burns, who was on top, was the first to his feet. He looked around for the goat, which was glaring at him malevolently. It lowered its head again.

Burns didn't try to open the gate. He jumped for the fence. His hands grabbed the top and his feet scratched for purchase on the weathered boards. A sharp pain ran up his back. He'd thought his tailbone was completely all right, and maybe it had been. But it wasn't now.

The goat charged. It missed Burns and hit the fence. There was a sound like a baseball bat hitting a tree.

The goat, addled by the collision, staggered around beneath Burns, who lost his grip on the fence and fell, landing on top of the goat, which emitted a weak "B-a-a-a-a-a-a" and didn't move.

Tomlin scrambled to his feet. "You've killed it. We've gotta get out of here."

He started to open the gate, but it was too late. Eric Holt and Dean Partridge were beside them. Holt had a flashlight, but it wasn't a cheap plastic one like the one Burns had been carrying. It was made of metal and it looked as if it would serve as a blackjack in a pinch.

"Stay where you are," Holt said. "We've called the police."

Partridge, who saw her animal companion on the ground, sank to her knees. "Billy," she said. "What have you done to Billy?"

"He hit his head," Burns told her, holding his back.

"Burns?" Holt said. "Is that you?"

Burns admitted that it was.

"What are you doing here?" Holt asked. He looked at Tomlin. "And who's that?"

Burns told him, then asked, "Have you really called the police?"

"No," Holt admitted, "but if you've killed Billy, Gwen will have your guts for garters."

Now that was an interesting picture, but one that Burns didn't care to contemplate. "I didn't hurt him. He just ran into the fence."

As Burns spoke, the goat suddenly recovered and jumped out of Partridge's arms. It shook its head, dashed across the yard, leaped atop the shed, and looked back at them.

Dean Partridge stood up. "I want to know what's going on here, Dr. Burns. I hope you and Dr. Tomlin have an explanation for this ridiculous invasion of my property."

"We have an explanation, all right," Tomlin said. "We know all about you two."

"There's nothing to know," Holt said. "I was merely discussing a curriculum problem with my academic dean."

"Sure you were," Tomlin said.

Holt hefted the flashlight. "You're being very insulting for a common housebreaker, Tomlin."

"There's no need for a fight," Burns said. "We were stupid to come here like this, but we do have an explanation."

"And what is it?" Holt asked.

"We know about Henry Mitchum," Burns said.

After they were in the house, all four of them sitting at the table, it didn't take Burns long to tell what he knew about Henry Mitchum. Tomlin tried hard not to look surprised as the story unfolded, but he obviously was. No matter how much he'd talked about "America's Most Wanted," he clearly was shocked to discover that he'd been right.

Almost as surprised as Burns was when Holt admitted, without any coaxing, that he was indeed Henry Mitchum.

After the admission, he leaned back in the straight-backed chair and relaxed. There was no tension in his face, and he was smiling.

"It feels good to say that, to get it out in the open after all these years," he told Burns. "You can't imagine what it's been like."

That was true. But Burns wanted to know how it had happened. Holt, or Mitchum, was glad to explain. It was as if he was glad to have someone to unburden himself to.

"I really didn't have anything to do with that bank robbery," he said. "It was just one of those terrible coincidences that no one would ever believe. I knew I'd go to prison, maybe even be executed. So when I had the chance to escape, I took it. You can't blame me for that."

Tomlin looked as if *he* could blame him, but Burns urged Holt to go on with the story.

"I disappeared into the underground," Holt said. "It was easy enough to do in those days, if you had the right contacts. I got a new identity, also easy enough. The real Eric Holt was killed in an automobile accident. So I got a copy of his birth certificate, and after that the rest was easy. I got a Social Security card and a driver's license and became Holt. Grew a beard and came to Texas. That's where I met Gwen."

Burns, whose tailbone was throbbing, was having trouble thinking of Dean Partridge as Gwen. "Did you meet her at Texas Tech?"

"That's right. I passed through Lubbock on my way to North Texas. I'd been told that the radical activity on those campuses wasn't so great as to draw much attention to them. I stayed in Lubbock for a few months with some friends of Gwen's. From there I wrote Holt's old high school and had his transcript sent to North Texas. I took the SAT under his name, passed, and enrolled as an overage freshman."

"I went to North Texas about that time," Tomlin said. "I don't remember ever seeing you there."

"About the only thing I did was go to classes, and when I was in them I sat in the back row and kept my mouth shut. I never went to the cafeteria, I never went to football games, I never even went to the library unless it was absolutely necessary. When I did, I went at times when there wasn't much activity. During football games, on Saturday mornings, times like that. I kept out of sight."

Tomlin nodded as if to say that explained things, which it probably did. Burns knew that Mal had undoubtedly gone to all the football games, and he wasn't the type to spend his Saturdays in the library.

"You pretty much know the rest, I suspect," Holt said to Burns. "I did well in school, stayed out of the limelight as much as possible, never went to any meetings. Things were fine until I came here."

There was only a slight accusatory tone to the latter remark, and Burns chose to overlook it. He wanted to know more about Holt's relationship with "Gwen," but he thought better of asking about it.

"Are you ready to come out of hiding now?" he asked.

Holt grinned wryly behind his beard. "I don't have much choice, do I?"

"Yeah, you do," Tomlin said. "You can go to jail for the murder of Tom Henderson."

Holt stiffened, and Dean Partridge looked outraged.

"I hope you don't think I had anything to do with that," Holt said.

"Well, we do," Tomlin said. "Henderson knew all about you, and you offed him."

" 'Offed' him?" Holt said.

"Yeah. Don't tell me you don't understand hippie talk."

Holt grinned. "I understand, all right, but I didn't off anyone. I was in Gwen's office when it happened."

"That's right," Dean Partridge said. "We were talking about Tom Henderson."

"What about him?" Burns asked.

"About what he knew," Holt said. "I was surprised to run into anyone from San Diego State in a place like this, but there he was. It took him a while to make the connection, but he remembered me."

Burns rubbed his greasepainted cheek. "Did he show you his yearbook?"

"Yes. Have you seen it?"

"I have it in my office. That's how I got onto you."

"Oh. Well, anyway, that's what we were talking about. I told Gwen that Henderson was on to me, and we were trying to decide what to do about it."

Tomlin was interested in that point. "So what did you decide?"

"We decided that I'd been in hiding long enough. There was no need to let Henderson go to the police. It was time for me to come out of hiding. You can't imagine what it's been like all these years, never telling anyone who I really am, never being able to talk to anyone, to trust anyone. I think that even if Henderson hadn't found me out, I would have cracked within the year."

"What about Gwe—uh, Dean Partridge?" Burns said. "You seem to be able to talk to her."

"We've corresponded over the years," Dean Partridge said. There was nothing in her voice to indicate that the correspondence was anything but that between two friends. "But sparingly. We thought this would finally be our chance to get together. And you can see how it's worked out."

"Not very well," Holt said. "Or maybe it has. One way or another I'll be free of the past now."

"But you were still interested in seeing the yearbook," Burns said. "You came to Henderson's office when I was searching it."

"Was that you?" Holt said. "I didn't know. I thought maybe it was the police. You scared me half to death. I never ran so fast in my life."

"I fell down the stairs," Burns said. He didn't mention his tailbone, which was still throbbing.

Tomlin was obviously disappointed in what he'd heard. "Okay, you went to look for the yearbook. But you say you didn't kill Henderson?"

"That's right."

"Damn," Tomlin said. "If you didn't, who did?"

Holt said, "I wish I could help you, but I don't have any idea."

"And neither do I," said Dean Partridge. "But I wish you'd find out, Dr. Burns."

"I'll try," he said.

Saying that she wanted to spare Billy any further trauma, Dean Partridge let Burns and Tomlin out the front door. Burns didn't much care about any possible trauma he might cause Billy, but he didn't even want to think about what another encounter might do for his aching tailbone.

As they walked through the den, Burns saw something sitting on a wooden game table. He detoured to look at it more closely.

"What's this?" he said, looking down.

"It's a fort made of Lincoln Logs," Dean Partridge said. "I collect things like that."

"And those little cavalrymen?"

"They're very authentic. I bought them from a man who makes his own molds. You can't get them in stores."

"Very nice," Burns said.

"Are you a collector, Dr. Burns?"

Burns didn't hear the dean's question. He was thinking.

"Dr. Burns? I asked if you were a collector."

"Oh," he said. "No. No I'm not. But that's a very nice fort, and those are wonderful soldiers. Such nice detail."

The dean smiled. "Thank you. I have others, if you'd like to see them."

"Some other time," Burns said, and he and Tomlin walked on to the door.

When they were outside, Tomlin asked, "What was that all about?"

"Never mind," Burns said, but he was smiling.

$\triangledown$

18

WHEN THEY WERE back in Burns's car, Tomlin lit up a Merit and took a deep drag.

"You know," he said, letting the smoke trickle out his mouth, "they may not be guilty of murder, but they're sure hypocrites."

"What do you mean?" Burns asked.

"All that political correctness crap we've been getting memos about. Did you see a single ashtray in the dean's house?"

Burns had to admit that he hadn't.

"Right. No smoking, just like at the school. Now if that's not discrimination, what is it?"

Burns didn't have a satisfactory answer.

"Of course you don't," Tomlin said. "They can drive us smokers underground, exactly as they claim Holt was driven underground, but that's just fine. Their freedoms are important, but ours aren't. I say it's hypocritical."

Burns thought Tomlin should get together with Boss Napier for a discussion of cultural Nazism. He said, "You may be right, but that's sort of beside the point."

Tomlin agreed. "Yeah. Do you think Holt's really going to turn himself in?"

"Yes. Don't you?"

"I guess he has to. If he doesn't, we will. Won't we?"

"Yes," Burns said. "We will."

Tomlin flicked ashes out the window. "The thing is, that won't get me off the hook with Napier, will it?"

"Probably not," Burns told him.

Tomlin sighed. "That's what I was afraid of."

Burns didn't sleep well at all that night.

Part of it was the pain in his tailbone, but that went away after he took a couple of aspirins. What wouldn't go away were his thoughts about Tom Henderson's murder.

Burns was convinced that Holt had nothing to do with it. His alibi was solid; Dean Partridge—Gwen—wasn't lying about her meeting with Holt in her office.

And Burns didn't really think that Kristi Albert would have killed Henderson because of the harassment she'd suffered. She was a typical student, more interested in her grades than in anything else. There was nothing particularly admirable in her attitude; in fact, she had been ready to blackmail Henderson, which wasn't to say he didn't deserve it. But at the last moment she hadn't gone through with it. Or so she said, and Burns believed her.

That left Walt Melling. Burns was sure that Melling had lied about one thing. He'd denied hitting Henderson, but the bruises on Henderson's face indicated that someone had struck him before his death. And Burns believed that someone was Walt Melling. He had the temper for it, and the fists.

While Burns hated to believe that Melling was a killer, there wasn't anyone else left on his list of suspects. That might not be a good reason for confronting Melling, but Burns had to do something. President Miller expected results by Monday, and Napier was pushing hard on Mal Tomlin. If Burns didn't find the killer, both Tomlin and Miller were going to be very disappointed.

Burns finally went to sleep wondering how to approach Melling. He dreamed of being stiff-armed all night long.

Burns took Elaine to lunch on Sunday, not only because he wanted to see her but also because he wanted to ask her advice. He went over the whole case with her, filling her in on everything he knew or guessed. She was fascinated by the story of Eric Holt.

"It's hard to believe that he could hide for so long," she said.

They were at the China Inn, and Elaine was daintily eating egg drop soup. Burns had wonton, and while he wasn't as dainty as Elaine, he was trying not to slurp.

"It wasn't so hard," he said. "The beard really changed his appearance—covered the weak chin and changed the whole shape of his face. After he graduated, he avoided going to meetings where he might run into anyone who knew him as Henry Mitchum, and he spent all his time at a little backwater school where it was highly unlikely he'd meet any of his friends from the old days. Of course he couldn't resist sending out his articles, but as long as no one met him or circulated his picture, he didn't have much to worry about."

"Still, to be a fugitive all that time . . ."

"He was tired of it, for sure. He's going to talk to Napier tomorrow and give himself up. It'll look good on Napier's record when he turns up someone who's been on the wanted lists for so long."

"But that still doesn't solve the murder, does it?" Elaine said.

Burns was about to agree when their waiter arrived with the main course—kung pao chicken for Burns, lemon chicken for Elaine. Better make that "server" rather than "waiter," Burns thought, though he wasn't sure why "server" was any better unless it was the fact that there had never been a serveress.

The server was a young man who had taken one of Burns's English classes. It always seemed a little incongruous to Burns when a person who on Friday came to class wearing old jeans, worn boots, and a ten-gallon hat turned up on Sunday serving Chinese food. Stereotyping again, Burns told himself. He had to do better.

When the server was gone, Burns said, "No, it doesn't solve the murder. That's what I wanted to ask you about."

While they ate, he went over his list of suspects with Elaine. They agreed that Holt could be eliminated, and they both thought that Kristi Albert wasn't a likely candidate.

"So that leaves Walt Melling," Burns said. "He has a real temper, no doubt about it. I've seen it in action. I suppose I should talk to him next."

"He said he was in his office, working on expense sheets?"

"Yes, and Dawn said he brought them home to work on them afterward. That seems a little cold-blooded to me, but then he didn't like Henderson. And maybe he killed him."

"And you want me to go with you when you talk to him," Elaine said.

Burns pushed away the remains of his kung pao chicken. "That's right. There shouldn't be any danger. I don't think he'll try anything if you're along."

The waiter came to take their plates away, leaving the check and two fortune cookies on a saucer.

"Don't you think R.M. would be better?" Elaine asked.

"I don't want to bring him into it yet. Not until I'm sure I have something. I was thinking that maybe we could trick Walt into admitting something."

"What if he doesn't have anything to admit?"

"He has to have something," Burns said. "Who else is there?"

Elaine reached toward the saucer with the fortune cookies. "Maybe we'll find an answer in these."

She picked up a cookie and broke it open, then pulled out the fortune and read it. " 'The wise man knows himself.' Is that Chinese?"

Burns didn't know. "Not specifically. It could be from any culture. The ancient Greeks believed it. So did Shakespeare. 'To thine own self be true.' *Hamlet*. And then there's Ralph Waldo Emerson. 'Trust thyself. Every heart vibrates to—' "

Elaine smiled. "I should have known not to ask an English teacher anything. What does yours say?"

Burns read it. " 'A little knowledge is a dangerous thing.' "

"Don't tell me," Elaine said. "I know that one. Alexander Pope?"

"Sort of," Burns said. "It's a misquotation, though. Pope said, 'A little *learning* is a dangerous thing.' And he qualified it by saying—"

Elaine held up her hand. "Never mind. I get the idea. Misquotations, *Hamlet*—you English teachers are always on the job."

"You sound a little like Boss Napier," Burns said.

"I wish you hadn't said that," Elaine told him.

"I won't say it again," Burns assured her, wondering why misquotations of Shakespeare and *Hamlet* were bouncing around in the back of his head as if they had something to do with the murder of Tom Henderson.

He thought about it as he paid the check, but he couldn't make any sense of it. Maybe it would come to him later. Now it was time to see if Walt Melling was at home.

Dawn Melling came to the door. She was wearing a baggy black sweatshirt and jeans that were neither black nor baggy. Burns tried not to stare.

"Hello, Dr. Burns," Dawn said. "And Ms. Tanner. What can I do for you?"

"We wanted to talk to Walt," Burns said. "Is he home?"

"He's in the den, watching some old fishing show," Dawn said. "Come on in."

They followed her into the den, where Walt was sitting on a couch that had a yellow afghan thrown across the back. He didn't look at them when they entered the room. He kept his eyes on the television set, where a man in a gimme cap was standing in the bow of a boat and casting a lure into a lake full of rotting tree stumps.

"Walt," Dawn said, "it's Dr. Burns and Ms. Tanner."

Walt still didn't look at them. It was as if he were mesmerized by the fishing show, where a large bass was now jumping out of the water on the end of the excited host's line.

"Walt," Dawn said. "Honey. There's someone here to see you."

Walt deigned to look away from the TV set as the fisherman knelt down, reached into the water, and grabbed the bass by the lip. "What do you want?" he asked.

"Just to talk," Burns said.

"I've talked to you all I'm going to talk." Melling turned back to his program.

"Walt!" Dawn said. "You know that's no way to behave."

"Why don't you and I go somewhere else and visit?" Elaine said. "We'll let Carl talk to your husband."

"No," Burns said. "I think she should be here."

Melling reached for a remote control and turned off the television set. Then he stood up and turned to Burns.

"I think you should be leaving," he said. His face was getting red.

"Not until you talk to me," Burns said, hoping that Melling wasn't going to hit him.

"Look," Melling began. "I don't have any intention—"

"Wait," Elaine said. "There's no need for you to be defensive, Mr. Melling. All Carl wants to do is ask you a few questions."

"That's right, Walt. Why are you so upset?" Dawn asked.

"Because he thinks I killed that idiot Tom Henderson," Melling told her. "And he's going to try to trick me into saying that I did."

"But you didn't," Dawn said. "You told me that you didn't have anything to do with it."

"You hit him, though," Burns said. "Didn't you, Walt?"

Walt's head snapped around. "Damn right I hit him. And I'd do it again. But I didn't kill him."

Well, that trick had worked. Catch the guy off guard and ask him a quick question that he's not expecting. Maybe he'll spit out an answer.

"Why did you lie to me earlier?" Burns asked.

Melling slammed a fist into the afghan on the back of the couch. The crocheted coverlet bounced up and settled back down.

"Because you think I killed that little geek," Walt said. "And I didn't. I can prove it."

"How?" Burns asked.

"I told you the other day. Someone went into Henderson's office after I did."

"You didn't say who that was," Burns pointed out.

"Because I don't know. But we can find out if we have to. I can find her picture in the yearbook and then we can ask her."

"I've already found her and talked to her."

Melling looked a little surprised. "Well, then. Now you know the truth."

"She says she doesn't remember seeing you."

"Then she's lying."

"I don't think so."

"She has to be. No wonder. She's probably the one who killed him."

"I don't believe that, either," Burns said.

Melling's face was getting redder and redder. He was getting ready to hit something again, and Burns was afraid that it wouldn't be the afghan this time.

"Calm down, honey," Dawn said. "You look like you're going to have a heart infraction."

Burns didn't ask what that might be. He agreed that Melling needed to calm down.

"She's right," Burns said. "If you're innocent, there's no need for you to act like this."

Melling took a deep, ragged breath and unclenched his fists. Then he sat down on the couch. Burns walked over and stood between him and the TV set.

"Look," Melling said. "If I killed Henderson, why did I tell you about that student? If I'd killed him, and if she'd gone into his office, she'd know what had happened. She could convict me easily. If I'd killed anyone, I would never have mentioned her."

"That's a point in your favor," Burns said. "But she didn't go into his office."

"How do you know that?"

"She told me."

"Maybe she's lying. Like I said, she's probably the one who killed him."

It was possible, maybe, but Burns didn't believe it. Still, Melling had a point. If he had killed Henderson, he wouldn't have mentioned Kristi. He didn't seem to know that she hadn't gone into Henderson's office.

"I just don't understand this," Dawn said. "I just don't understand it at all."

Burns didn't understand it either. It was beginning to look as if none of his suspects was guilty. And that just wasn't possible. *Someone* had murdered Tom Henderson. At least that was what Boss Napier thought, and he had convinced Burns.

"Maybe I should put on some music," Dawn said. "That might present a better atmosphere."

Burns wasn't sure how music could present an atmosphere, but something clicked in his brain.

"Music hath charms to soothe the savage breast," he said, though Dawn had said "breasts" when he'd talked to her earlier.

"That's so true," Dawn said, moving toward the CD player atop the TV set.

But Burns wasn't interested in the truth or falsity of the quotation. He was interested in the circumstances in which he'd last been reminded of it. A lot of connections were being made in his head.

"Wait a minute, Dawn," he said. "Do you remember that day in your office when we were talking about the time Tom Henderson said something . . . inappropriate to you?"

Dawn blushed and glanced sideways at Walt. "Yes," she whispered. "I remember that."

"Good. When I said something about Walt's knowing what Henderson had done, you asked me a question. You said, 'Did you tell Walt?' Remember?"

Dawn screwed up her face in thought. "I guess I remember that. Why?"

"Because I thought *you* told him."

"Well, I didn't." Dawn looked more directly at her husband, who seemed to have no idea what was going on. "I know how he gets when he's mad. I would never tell him about a thing like that. There's just no telling what he might do."

"Great, Dawn," Melling said. "Now Burns will be *really* convinced that I killed the little twerp."

"No," Burns said. "I'm not convinced of that at all. But I think I might know who did kill him. The person who told you about what he said to Dawn."

"And who would that be?" Elaine asked.

"I don't know," Dawn said. "But I know *I* didn't."

"And neither did I," Burns said. "So that means someone else told him. Tell us who it was, Walt."

And Walt did.

19

"I SHOULD HAVE known," Burns said. "I can't believe I didn't figure it out."

"Don't blame yourself," Elaine said. "Besides, you could be wrong."

"I don't think so. I've been wrong all along, but this time I'm right."

Burns drove past the HGC library, turned into the drive, and pulled behind the building to the front of the boiler room. The door was open, and Burns could see Dirty Harry tipped back in his chair, his feet propped against the wall.

"I'm going to talk to him for a second," Burns said. "You wait here."

The old watchman was probably sound asleep, but that just made him all the more dangerous. If he was awakened suddenly, he might draw his pistol and pull the trigger before he knew what he was doing.

"Don't surprise him," Elaine said.

"I'll try not to," Burns told her, slamming the Plymouth door as hard as he could.

The noise echoed throughout the boiler room, and Dirty Harry sat upright, the legs of his chair banging on the floor. He looked around wildly, as if half convinced that the boiler had exploded and sent him to heaven. Just in case it hadn't and there was some other threat to his life, his hand scrabbled for the butt of his pistol.

"It's just me," Burns yelled. "Carl Burns!"

Dirty Harry's eyes came to rest on Burns and he stopped fumbling for the sidearm.

"What do you want around here on a Sunday?" he asked. He laughed wheezily. "You come to smoke a cigarette?"

"I just wanted to talk," Burns said, entering the boiler room. "About the night Tom Henderson died."

Dirty Harry settled back into his chair. "Terrible thing. I've known Tom Henderson ever since he first came on this campus, nearly twenty years ago."

Burns agreed that Henderson's death was a terrible thing.

"Where were you that night?" Burns asked.

"Wasn't night, exactly. Just gettin' on toward dark, is what it was."

"Right. But where were you?"

"Makin' my rounds," Dirty Harry said. "Same thing ever' day. 'Round about closin' time, I check all the buildin's, make sure what's supposed to be locked is locked and what's supposed to be open is open."

Burns had thought that was the case. He saw Dirty Harry nearly every Tuesday evening as the watchman went through Main on his rounds, shaking the door handles and peering into the locked offices.

"So you were in Main that night?"

"Wasn't night," Dirty Harry said. "It was evenin'."

"Evening. Right. Were you there?"

"Sure enough was. Always am, 'round that time."

Now came the part that Burns was guessing at. "And were you the one who some student sent to get Henderson's wife?"

"That's right. Sure hated to be the one to tell her. Known her long's I've known him."

"*Did* you tell her?"

Dirty Harry gave Burns a look. "Now what's that supposed to mean?"

"I mean, she teaches in the business building. Did you have any trouble finding her?"

Dirty Harry was getting suspicious. "How'd you know that?"

"I didn't know it for sure. I just thought that might be what happened."

"I don't see what difference it makes."

"No difference," Burns said. "I just wondered if she was in her office."

"Well, no. She wasn't there. But she came in right after I got there. Why?"

"It was just something I was wondering about," Burns said. "Was she carrying anything?"

"Just her book bag that I remember. She was real broke up when I told her about her husband."

"I'm not surprised. Well, that's all I wanted to know. Thanks for talking to me."

Burns turned to leave.

Dirty Harry called him. "Dr. Burns?"

Burns turned back. "What?"

"She's gonna catch y'all. You know that, don't you?"

"Who do you mean?"

"That new dean. She's gonna find out y'all are smokin' in here and there's gonna be hell to pay."

Burns thought it over. "You're not going to tell her, are you?"

Dirty Harry laughed. The laugh had a phlegmy sound. "Not me, son. If you was to break in one of the buildin's, or park illegally, I'd squeal. But not about smokin'."

"Then maybe she won't find out," Burns said.

"You wish," Dirty Harry said.

Elaine thought it was time to call Napier, but Burns didn't agree.

"We don't have any proof," he said. "We've got to get the evidence."

"What evidence?"

Burns pulled the shift lever and put the Plymouth in drive. "You'll see," he said.

*   *   *

It was a little past midafternoon when they arrived at Samantha Henderson's house in the Heights. Burns rang the doorbell.

This time it took even longer for Samantha to answer the ring than it had the first time they'd visited her. And she looked, if anything, worse than she had then. She had fixed her hair for the funeral, but it hadn't been touched since. And she didn't look as if she'd slept.

Burns thought he knew why.

Just as before, Samantha stood inside the house, looking out at them, not inviting them to enter.

This time it was Elaine who said, "Can we come in?"

"Why not?" Samantha stepped back, opening the door wide enough for them to come inside.

Burns looked at the living room. It wasn't much dirtier than it had been, but the odor of decay seemed a little stronger. The overstuffed chair was still tipped to one side.

Samantha stood listlessly in the middle of the room and looked at them, but she had nothing to say.

Burns didn't know exactly where to begin, either. He looked at Elaine.

"Why don't you sit down, Samantha?" Elaine said.

Samantha shook her head. Her hair fell around her face. "Don't want to."

"We have to talk to you," Burns said. "It's about Tom."

"What about him? He's dead."

"We know that." Burns decided to try the shock treatment. It had gotten an admission out of Melling. "And we know that you killed him."

He didn't know what kind of reaction he'd expected. Maybe, he'd thought, Samantha would break down and cry. Or maybe she would confess.

He certainly didn't think she would attack him.

But she did. She flew across the room, her fingers shaped into talons, her wild hair flying.

"Liar! Liar!" she yelled, and then she smashed into Burns,

throwing him to the floor and scratching at his face with both hands, yelling "Liar!" all the while.

Burns tried to throw her off, but she was stronger than he was. He tried to grab her wrists, but she was too fast for him. All he could do was deflect her from his eyes, though she succeeded in inflicting several scratches on his face.

He heard Elaine saying, "Stop it! Stop it!" and he was pretty sure that she was trying to drag Samantha off him, but it wasn't working.

He was giving himself up for a goner when Elaine pulled Samantha's head back and cracked her on the chin with a credible right cross.

Samantha was stunned, but she wasn't out. She jumped off Burns, twisted around, and launched herself at Elaine, wrestling her to the floor and grabbing her hair. She pounded Elaine's head into the rug three times before Burns could get to her.

He grabbed her arms and pulled her away from Elaine. She writhed in his hands like a snake, twisting her head back to spit at him. Burns was like the man who didn't know what to do with the tiger now that he had caught it.

She kicked backward and hit his shin. He let go of her arms. She dropped on top of Elaine, grabbed her hair again, and started banging her head on the rug.

Every time her head hit the floor, Elaine said something that sounded like "Uh."

Burns didn't want to hit Samantha. It didn't seem politically correct. But he couldn't think of anything else to do. He grabbed a cushion off the couch and slammed it into the side of her head as hard as he could.

She slid off Elaine and whirled on him like a catamount. He whacked her in the face with the cushion. He hit her again and again, until she collapsed to the rug, crying.

It was probably a sad picture, but right at the moment Burns had no sympathy for her. He put the cushion back on the couch and helped Elaine to her feet.

"I tried to stop her," Elaine said. "But I couldn't."

"It's not your fault," Burns said. "I shouldn't have provoked her."

"Your face is bleeding," Elaine told him. She opened her purse and took out a tissue. "Hold still."

Burns tried to be brave while she blotted his face. Samantha huddled on the floor, crying.

"We should look for some alcohol to put on these scratches," Elaine said.

"Later," Burns said.

He walked over to the recliner and tipped it up. There was a canvas book bag under it. Burns pulled the bag out and let the chair back down to the floor. The bag was turned inside out, and it was quite heavy.

That was because it was holding a notebook, a typing text, and a bust of Sigmund Freud. The inside of the bag was stained dark with blood, and the odor of decay was a lot stronger.

"She put the bust in the bag, then swung it and hit him," Burns said.

"But R.M. didn't notice any marks like that," Elaine said.

"She hit him in the back of the head. Then the back of his head hit the sidewalk."

"Oh."

Burns walked over to Samantha, who was sitting up now.
"Isn't that about right, Samantha?" he said.

She rubbed her eyes with the back of her hand. "Yes. I'd gone by to speak to him about his behavior with Dawn Melling. He blamed me because Walt Melling had hit him. He yelled at me, and then he turned his back on me and told me to get out of his office. I wanted to hurt him, so I put that awful bust in my bag and hit him with it." She started crying again. "I didn't know he'd go out the window."

Maybe she was telling the truth, Burns thought.

Maybe not.

"So it was all Elaine's idea," Boss Napier said. "She gets the credit."

"That's right," Burns told him.

They were sitting in Samantha Henderson's living room, but Samantha wasn't there. She was on her way to the city jail.

"Tell me how I solved it," Elaine said.

Burns was glad to. "You reminded me of misquotations and *Hamlet*. And there was something you said about sexual harassment."

"I understand the misquotations part. But not the *Hamlet*."

" 'The lady doth protest too much.' "

"I get it," Napier said. "She was the one who was jealous. All those women, they didn't come on to her husband at all. She was—what do you call it?—in denial."

"Close enough," Burns said, though he wasn't a psychologist. "She was jealous, and she knew what he was doing, but she couldn't admit to anyone that her husband was a philanderer. She tried to pretend that it was someone else's fault. If anyone asked her about what was going on, she blamed the women."

"That's a real English teacher word," Napier said. " 'Philanderer.' "

"I mean he played around."

"I know what you mean. I was just talking about the word."

"Right. But it's probably the wrong word. I don't think he really played around. I think he just talked. And touched."

"That's the sexual harassment part," Elaine said. "What did I say about harassment that gave Samantha away?"

"That was the most important thing," Burns said. "Not that I agree with it."

"Agree with *what*?"

"That it's always the woman who suffers. You said that after we talked to Kristi Albert."

"And you don't agree with that?" Elaine said.

"I don't," Napier said. "Look at Henderson."

Elaine gave Napier a look. "I didn't mean that kind of suffering."

"Tom suffered in other ways," Burns said. "He had a real

problem. He should have gotten help. Maybe I should have said something to him about it. I knew what was going on, and I kept my mouth shut."

"That's the trouble with men," Elaine said. "You never think of talking about something. But that's beside the point now. I can see why my saying that made you think of Samantha."

"Yes. She'd controlled herself pretty well for a long time, but somehow she heard about Dawn Melling. Maybe Tom even told her."

"I wouldn't put it past someone like that," Elaine said.

"I wouldn't either. She didn't know what to do about it any more than I did, though. So she told Walt. She thought maybe he'd take care of it."

"Maybe he did," Napier said. "Maybe a little thrashing was what Henderson needed."

Elaine was disdainful. "You men think that's the answer to everything."

"Hey," Napier said, "I said *maybe*."

Elaine didn't respond, so Napier turned to Burns. "I have to hand it to you, Burns. You did it again."

"I guess I did," Burns said, wondering why he didn't feel better about it. "But that's not all."

"There's more?" Napier said. "Don't tell me your buddies are guilty too."

"It's not that. It's something entirely different."

Napier frowned. "I'm not sure I like the sound of that."

"You'll love it," Burns said. "How would you like to be famous? Maybe even get yourself on television?"

"How am I going to do that?"

"You're going to accept the surrender of Henry Mitchum."

"Hot damn," Napier said.

20

Burns could see that Franklin Miller was torn.

On the one hand, the surrender of Henry Mitchum/Eric Holt to Boss Napier was going to bring the school national publicity, though not exactly the kind of publicity that Miller coveted.

On the other hand, the news about Holt completely overshadowed the scandalous murder of Tom Henderson by his own wife, which would otherwise have dominated the Pecan City news and quite possibly have spread to Texas's larger cities.

The news about Holt also overshadowed the student court's hearing on the matter of George (The Ghost) Kaspar's guilt or innocence on charges of looksism, and Miller had to be grateful for that. No one was going to worry about a minor case of political incorrectness when one of the nation's most sought-after fugitives was being booked in the local cop shop.

"What do you think will happen to him?" Miller asked Burns.

They were meeting in Miller's office before George's hearing.

"I think he'll get off," Burns said. "It's been a long time, he's led an exemplary life, and he still says he didn't have a thing to do with the bank robbery. He was just in the wrong place at the wrong time."

"I hope you're right," Miller said. "It won't look good for HGC if he's convicted."

"The school won't be hurt even if that happens," Burns said. "No one here knew who he was, except for Dean Partridge, and she's the one who convinced him to come here and turn himself in."

That was the story they had decided on, at any rate. It was true enough, as such stories went.

"He was at another school for a long time," Miller said. "He didn't turn himself in while he was there."

Burns nodded. "Right. It took HGC to persuade him to do that. If anything, we'll come out of this looking like the good guys."

"Excellent," Miller said, rubbing his hands together. "You've done a fine job, Burns, solving the murder and getting Holt to give himself up all at the same time. By the way, who's going to be teaching Holt's classes?"

"The judge may let him finish the semester," Burns said. "Let's wait and see."

Miller beamed. "Excellent. Now, what are you going to do about George Kaspar?"

"That one could be tricky," Burns admitted.

The student government met and rendered judgment in a small room that had once been HGC's faculty lounge. The room wasn't big enough to hold all the spectators at the hearing, and Burns had to shove his way through a knot of students to get inside.

The five students on the court were sitting at a small rectangular table in the center of the room. George (The Ghost) Kaspar, looking as pale as his cartoon counterpart, was there, too, as was Bunni. Elaine was sitting in a chair on one side of the room, and there were several other faculty members in attendance as well. Mal and Earl were sitting near Elaine, and the Mellings were beside them. The room buzzed with conversation.

Burns wondered if this scene was a preview of many like it to come, not at HGC but all around the country. He knew that one college was adopting a sort of Miranda warning for sex on dates and that every single step in the relationship had to be agreed to in advance. He imagined solemn students with laminated cards in their hands checking off every move: "May I touch this strap? You have the right to remain silent. If you choose to remain silent, I will take that to mean that I may not touch that strap."

And so it would go for every strap, buckle, and zipper. God knows whose passion could survive the undressing for the even more intimate moments. Or moments that had once been intimate. Being sure to follow the checklist would probably cool even the most ardent passions. Burns didn't like to think about it.

George appeared glad to see Burns, almost as if he thought Burns was the only friend he had in the room.

Burns walked over to stand behind George's chair, leaned forward, and slipped a piece of paper in George's hand. He didn't think anyone saw him.

"What's this?" George asked. He sounded as if he had been hoping for Al Pacino and the flamethrower, for which a piece of paper was a poor substitute.

Burns said, "It's another poem. Ask if you can have a word with Bunni. If she'll talk to you, tell her you have something for her. Then give her the poem."

George looked around the room. All the chairs were full, and students were standing wherever they could get a view of the table.

He looked back at Burns. "It was a poem that got me into all this," he said.

Burns said he knew that. "But this is different. It's worth a shot."

George wasn't the picture of confidence, but he said, "All right."

He leaned over to Rodney Black, the student who was to preside at the meeting, and whispered something to him. Rodney nodded and bent across the table to speak to Bunni.

Burns couldn't hear what they were saying over the buzz, but he saw Bunni nod. Rodney motioned for George to go ahead and talk to her.

"Tell her you read the poem, and it reminded you of her," Burns said in George's ear.

George nodded and got up. He walked around to Bunni's chair and handed her the piece of paper. Bunni unfolded it and looked at the poem. George whispered something, and she blushed.

It's up to you now, George, Burns thought, hoping George would know what to say. Apparently he did. He continued to talk, and Bunni continued to listen. After a minute or so, the conversation ended and George returned to his seat.

"How'd it go?" Burns asked.

"We'll see," George said, and they did.

Bunni stood up and said she wasn't interested in pursuing the charge of looksism. "It was all a big mistake. I misunderstood George, and I'd like to apologize to him right now, in front of everyone. He never based his opinion of me on my appearance. I know that now. I'd also like to apologize to the members of the student court for wasting their time."

Then she walked through the crowd and out of the room. George got up and followed her. Burns thought they'd be just fine.

"What was that you gave George?" Elaine asked as they were leaving the building. "I saw you slip him that paper."

"It was a poem," Burns said. "It reminded him of Bunni. And it reminded me of you. I just happen to have another copy."

He took a paper out of his pocket and handed it to Elaine.

" 'Hymn to Intellectual Beauty,' " he said. "Shelley."

Elaine smiled. "You think you're pretty smart, don't you?"

"One of the Romantics started all this," Burns said. "I thought it would be appropriate if another of them finished it. And it looks as if it might have worked."

Elaine took his arm. "Yes, I guess it did, even if Shelley wasn't talking about a particular person's intellectual beauty."

"Who said he was?" Burns asked.

"Never mind. By the way, Mal Tomlin said something about forming a faculty baseball team."

"That's right," Burns said. "I'm going to play second base. I hope you'll watch some of the games." He thought how that must sound. "Unless you want to play, of course. I'm sure there are a few openings on the team."

"I think I'll just watch," she said, and Burns hoped he wouldn't make a fool of himself on an infield fly.

They neared Burns's car. Someone was standing beside it. Boss Napier.

"What a pleasant surprise," Burns said. "Don't tell me there's been another murder that I'm going to have to solve for you."

"You know what I'm here for, Burns," Napier said.

"That's where you're wrong. I don't have any idea."

"And I'm Little Orphan Annie."

"Well, *I* don't know what you're here for," Elaine said. "Will someone please tell me what's going on?"

"Lincoln Logs," Napier said, and Burns grinned.

Napier saw the grin. "And lead soldiers. Damn you, Burns, that's why you had Holt give himself up at Cartilage's house, isn't it."

"Partridge," Burns said. "You might want to get used to it."

"She wears hippie glasses," Napier said. "She doesn't even wear lipstick."

"True," Burns said. "But she collects Lincoln Logs. It's a relationship made in heaven."

"I'll get you for this, Burns," Napier said.

"Maybe," Burns said.

And maybe not, he thought.